Their mouths met in an accidental kiss—a faux pas which might have been easily rectified if Jess had apologised immediately and created some distance. Except Rob's lips were as soft as they looked, and she lingered there a little longer than was probably socially acceptable.

'Sorry.' She stepped back when common sense kicked in again. Kissing Rob when all he'd done was be nice to her was a stupid, impulsive move which screamed desperation.

Rob shot out his hand to catch her around the waist and pull her back. She was mid-gasp and flush against him when his mouth came crashing back down on hers.

He stole her breath away as he caught her bottom lip between his and sent her head spinning from the lack of oxygen. She didn't know where the unexpected display of passion had come from, but she wanted more.

The sensation of butterfly wings on her skin tickled her from head to toe, until every erogenous zone in her body was on high alert. She really shouldn't be enjoying this as much as she was. He was grieving. She was a mess. But this felt so good…

Dear Reader,

As a mother, I know that feeling of helplessness when my sons suffer any sort of illness or injury. For those whose young children have been struck by cancer it must be even more difficult to stay strong. It's a devastating disease which affects the whole family.

The research I did for this book taught me a lot about the patients and staff who inhabit the oncology wards. There are some amazing stories of courage and determination out there, along with some truly heartbreaking tales. However, one thing is clear—thanks to the ongoing research carried out in this field, survival rates are higher than ever.

My glamorous heroine, Jessica, is a survivor of childhood leukaemia herself. She's keen for her documentary to show the amazing work that goes on behind the scenes of cancer treatment, but finds opposition in Rob, a fiercely private oncologist. Behind their successful careers both are grieving losses of their own, but they can't hide for ever when they're working together in such an emotional environment.

I loved writing this book, even though the subject matter was so difficult it brought me to tears on more than one occasion. I have nothing but respect for the families and staff who deal with this illness every day. I will be making a donation to my local children's hospice from the proceeds of this book.

Love,

Karin x

A KISS
TO CHANGE
HER LIFE

BY
KARIN BAINE

First published in Great Britain 2016
By Mills & Boon, an imprint of HarperCollins*Publishers*
1 London Bridge Street, London, SE1 9GF

© 2016 Karin Baine

ISBN: 978-0-263-26349-7

Our policy is to use papers that are natural, renewable and recyclable
products and made from wood grown in sustainable forests. The logging
and manufacturing processes conform to the legal environmental
regulations of the country of origin.

Printed and bound in Great Britain
by CPI Antony Rowe, Chippenham, Wiltshire

Karin Baine lives in Northern Ireland with her husband, two sons, and her out-of-control notebook collection. Her mother and grandmother's vast collection of books inspired her love of reading and her dream of becoming a Mills & Boon author. It wasn't until she joined her critical group UCW that she started to believe she could actually write—and only her husband's support enabled her to pursue it. At least now she can tell people she has a *proper* job! You can follow Karin on Twitter: @karinbaine1.

Another book by Karin Baine

Mills & Boon Medical Romance

French Fling to Forever

Visit the Author Profile page
at millsandboon.co.uk for more titles.

For my bestie, Cathy. I still owe you a Mr G story!

A huge thanks to Charlotte Mursell
for working so hard with me on this book.
My afternoon with you and Laura McCallen
is one I'll remember for a long time. xx

I also need to give a shout-out to Brian and AJ,
who helped me with the technical stuff. Even though
I may have taken a few creative liberties with it…

CHAPTER ONE

THE BANK OF monitors filled with Dr Dreamboat's handsome profile as he strode past the remote camera in the hospital corridor. Jessica could see why the female members of the production team, and some of the men, had bestowed the nickname upon him. His strong stubbled jawline, wavy dark hair and piercing blue eyes made Rob Campbell perfect eye candy. With the rolled-up sleeves of his shirt bunched at his biceps and his sand-coloured trousers taut across muscled thighs, the guy looked as if he should be playing rugby and smashing into other huge beasts rather than holding hands with poorly children. As the consultant paediatric oncologist at the Belfast Community Children's Hospital, he was a vital link between the patients, staff and camera crew. It was a shame he'd been so reluctant for the documentary series to go ahead in the first place.

He'd voiced his considerable concern that they were violating his patients' privacy at the production meetings and it was in the project's best interest for Jessica to get him on board. Regardless of the hospital board's decision to allow filming and the crew's assurances that they would be sympathetic and respectful to all involved, the consultant had treated their presence here with quiet disdain. Jessica hadn't addressed him directly in the few days they'd been on-site to prepare for filming and instead had focused on building a rapport with the families on the ward. She had the signed consent forms of those willing to participate and didn't want anything to jeopardise everything she'd worked towards. This meant more to her than ratings and job security.

Cancer had been a huge part of her life; it still was in some ways. Not content to hijack her childhood, it had also tried to dictate her future. The after-effects of her treatment had followed her into adulthood and triggered early menopause. Just as she'd started to recover her femininity, that life-stealing illness had dealt the ultimate blow and made sure she could never be a whole woman.

Well, cancer had taken on the wrong redheaded warrior to tango with. It could take away her fiancé who couldn't deal with a barren future wife. It could take away the daughter she'd always dreamed of pampering like a little princess. But it couldn't take away her spirit. Nor anyone else's if she could possibly help it. If this series brought more funding to the hospital and helped even one child with their fight, it would be worth the pain it caused Jessica to relive her own.

The easiest way to allay Dr Campbell's fears that they'd trample over anyone in the pursuit of a good story would be to explain she was a survivor of childhood leukaemia herself. It would substantiate her plea that she simply wanted to raise public awareness of the incredible work that went on here. But that would mean exposing her weakness and the last time she'd done that it had cost her everything.

Adam, the man she'd thought she'd spend the rest of her life with, simply hadn't been able to cope with her health problems and who could blame him? When a man proposed to a vibrant young woman, he didn't expect to be marrying some prematurely aged, decrepit version of her. Their engagement had ended once Jessica's failings as a woman had become apparent. The hot flushes, mood swings and childless future had been difficult enough for her to deal with, never mind live alongside.

In tear-filled hindsight, he probably hadn't been the right man for her. Although he'd been right when he'd told her no man should be expected to take her on now that she was infertile. It would be selfish of her to ask that of anyone, not to mention detrimental to her well-being to imagine it a possibility. She'd only got through her body's changes and the break-up by accepting her fate as an eternal singleton and moving on. These days, her career was her significant other and these programmes filled that void where a family should be. They were her babies and she cherished every one. Each successful production she made was validation of her worth and all that she needed to fill her life. No man could ever make her feel as good as the awards and accolades bestowed on her for her work to date.

Now, not even an uncooperative oncologist could persuade her to divulge that deeply personal medical information lest it be used against her in some way. She'd worked too hard to put the pain of the past behind her to use it as a bargaining tool.

This was the first day of shooting and Jessica wanted to get it off to the best start possible. She'd done some reading up on Dr Campbell, enough to understand where his passion lay, and it wasn't a million miles from her own. He was leading the fundraising drive to pay for an MRI scanner for the Children's Hospital. There was no reason they couldn't use the airtime to promote the cause and perhaps cultivate a more harmonious relationship at the same time.

With that in mind, Jessica left the busy hub of the mobile production unit situated in the grounds of the hospital car park and went in search of her latest challenge. She'd learned at an early age to meet every obstacle in her path head-on and Rob Campbell was no exception. A liberal application of lip gloss, and a toss of her bouncy auburn curls later, she was ready to make contact with her target. She strode through the hospital entrance with a confidence that wasn't one hundred per cent genuine.

It was still early morning, the best time to do a recce around the corridors while it was relatively peaceful, quiet except for the sharp tap of her stilettos on the tiled floor. The impending sense of doom which descended as she navigated the maze of corridors had less to do with first-day nerves and everything to do with her residual hospital phobia.

The bright, airy atmosphere of the modern hospital was a far cry from the imposing Victorian building she'd attended for treatment. Instead of dark and imposing corridors, this wing was lined with colourful frescos designed to appeal to the children who attended.

Despite the visual differences and the time she'd had to get used to the surroundings, the glare of fluorescent lights and smell of bleach and antiseptic still took her back to a time when she wasn't so in control of her own destiny. Her steps faltered as a tide of nausea washed over her and forced a halt to her journey. She leaned against the wall, fighting to regulate her breathing and quell her rebelling stomach.

Inhale. Count to five. Exhale. Try not to puke on

your expensive red-soled shoes. Repeat until normal brain function returns.

Jessica pulled off her heels so her stockinged feet rested flat on the cool floor, back on solid ground. This wasn't about her. She was a visitor this time around, a grown-up replacing that pitiful figure who'd once resided here. When she'd first heard about this opportunity, she'd jumped at the chance to take part, regardless of her personal experience, perhaps even because of it.

Good or bad, hospital life had been a huge part of her childhood. Without the staff who'd looked after her, she would never have made it past adolescence, never mind the ripe old age of twenty-eight. Finally, she was in a position to pay something back. Replacing a husband and two point four kids with an impressive CV and impeccable professional reputation meant she could shine a light on a worthy cause. Nothing was going to stand in the way of that. Not her own personal issues and certainly not a difficult doctor who didn't know the first thing about her.

The double doors at the end of the corridor swung open and closed as staff walked in and out, giving a quick flash of the elusive consultant in his natural habitat. Every glimpse of Tall-Dark-and-Handsome reminded her how he'd earned his hospital heart-throb status. The nurses were flitting around him like groupies around a rock star and she was sure there were a few hoping to catch his eye for more than professional reasons. She could see why his good looks and high-ranking position seemed to attract every female within a five-mile radius but Jessica's focus had to remain on her project. There was no time for distractions. Certainly not a sexy, six-foot-plus real-life superhero one.

She gave herself a mental shake and coaxed her mind

away from the image of her new work colleague in body-hugging Lycra and tights. Fantasy rarely lived up to reality anyway.

With another deep breath, she drew herself up to her full five feet eight inches and made her way towards him, her shoes still in hand. Since any infection was potentially life-threatening to those on the other side of the doors, she paused only to squirt some hand sanitiser from the dispenser on the wall before she entered the ward.

Dr Campbell was standing at the nurses' station, his back to her, exuding a don't-come-any-closer authority without even trying. It took every ounce of her courage to edge closer to him.

'What do you want?' He didn't look up from the charts he was studying as he barked at her. It was the tone a busy and important professional used to fend off time-wasters so that only the bravest souls would persevere with their queries. She used it herself from time to time.

Having seen him in action on the ward from a distance, she knew how tender he could be under different circumstances. Clearly he didn't intend to make friends with her any time soon. Jessica reminded herself she'd taken on much worse than a doctor with a chip on his shoulder and lived to tell the tale.

'Hi. I'm Jessica Halliday, a producer for the documentary series currently being filmed. I was hoping we could have a quick chat before filming gets underway.'

'No can do. I have a full schedule this morning, even if I thought there was any point in speaking to you.' That gruff Scottish accent could've reduced a lesser mortal to a puddle of hormones, or tears. Not this girl. She didn't do swooning. Although when he did eventually turn around she might have shivered a tiny bit under his blue steel stare.

'It's important the viewers see the stories from the staff point of view as well as the patients'. I really think we could both benefit from working together and, as the man in charge, your input means a lot to the show.' As much as it galled her to sacrifice her pride, she wasn't averse to using flattery in order to get his approval.

'I'm sure there are a lot of men who would bend over backwards to keep you happy, Ms Halliday.' The doctor swept his gaze over her and, to her horror, a tingle of awareness danced across her skin. Male appreciation wasn't unfamiliar to her when a busy lifestyle ensured she kept her slim figure. However, she wasn't in the market for an inflexible male, and she didn't appreciate her body trying to convince her otherwise.

'I have no interest in reality television. If I did, I'd audition for one of those singers' got-no-talent shows instead of piggybacking on the misfortunes of the sick for celebrity status. I've consented to filming—that doesn't mean I'll pretend to be happy about it. These kids are going through enough without having cameras and microphones shoved in their faces. Now, if you'll excuse me, I have patients to see.' He broke off eye contact and returned to shuffling his paperwork.

The visual dismissal was the human equivalent of being hit with a fly swatter. Thanks to one life-altering break-up, Jessica didn't take rejection well. Her self-esteem demanded she leave more of an impression than an indistinguishable smudge in his day.

She shot out her hand to still his and demand attention. If she'd imagined him to feel like the cold fish he'd portrayed, the heat burning her fingertips where she touched him told her otherwise. Before she could linger on that thought, he snatched his hand away, frowned and took a step away from her as though she was contagious.

The snub stung like a sunburn in a hot shower. From her expensive clothes habit to her regular beauty treatments, she worked hard to make an impression on people. And to feel good in her own skin. She couldn't help but take any unwarranted slight against her personally and there was only one way to soothe the burn. With cool, hard facts.

'I'm sorry you feel that way about what we are trying to do here. For the record, this is *not* a reality show— it's a factual documentary series. As we explained before, our intention is to provide an accurate record of the process here and how serious illness affects the lives of everyone involved. I'll have to interview the staff and patients, so we'll need to draw up a schedule... I know there's a disused storeroom we can use for that once it's cleaned up... It would be great if we can organise a team meeting between my crew and yours every morning to coordinate filming. I hope we can find a way to work together, Dr Campbell, because I would really like to help—'

'I think you're under the misapprehension that we're somehow colleagues. I am not here to make your job easier, but to ensure my patients receive the best care available. For their sake I hope you don't get in the way of that.' He swept the files under his arm in one smooth motion and started to walk away before she had a chance to mention the MRI scanner.

As if sensing her mentally swearing at him, the consultant turned back. 'And please put your shoes on and at least try to be professional here.'

With her livelihood on a collision course with his ego, Jessica hopped across the floor after him, desperately trying to wedge her shoes back on her feet. As the go-to person on these productions, she didn't normally get flustered. She was the cool one in a crisis. Until now. She put it down to the surroundings rather than being nervous around this particular man.

'I am trying to be professional, if you would only cooperate.'

He stopped, arched a mocking eyebrow at her as she bobbed about like an inebriated socialite falling out of a nightclub, and walked on. She'd underestimated the strength of his objection and his unease was going to be even more noticeable on camera. She needed to fix this. Fast.

'I want to help with the fundraising for the MRI scanner.'

That soon stopped him in his tracks and he turned to face her.

'How?'

It seemed her determination had paid off as she located his Achilles heel. At least now she had an opening for a more civil conversation. She hoped.

'We can flash up the details of where people can donate on screen during the programme. Do you have a website set up?'

'Yes, but I suspect you already know that.' He watched her through narrowed eyes. So much for getting him onside. Now he was looking at her as if she was some kind of stalker.

She shrugged. 'I make no apologies for doing my research. This comes down to the fact that we can give the cause a boost.'

'If I play nice?'

'We appear to have got off on the wrong foot, Doctor. I'm not here to bully people into doing what I want. I'm simply trying to do right by all the families here. The scanner appeal will get a mention whether or not we can get along.' Jessica could produce a stunning programme in the worst of circumstances but she could do without this, frankly uncalled for, animosity when there were already so many emotional threads tying her to this.

'Don't take it personally. I'm very protective of my patients, as I'm sure you can imagine.'

'Of course. But we're on the same team here. Why don't we start again? I'm Jessica.' She held out her hand and attempted to erase their first frosty introduction.

The Highland Terror began to thaw as he gave her a smile capable of breaking the hearts of every hot-blooded woman in the vicinity. Thankfully, Jessica didn't let hers make decisions for her any more. These days she kept that vital organ out of her relationships with men and kept everything strictly casual. It was the only defence she had against the pain which would inevitably follow if she got too involved. Short and sweet was the way she ran her love life. That way there was no pressure on her to reveal her unsuitability as a prospective wife and mother further down the line.

'Rob.' He clapped his large hand into hers to shake on the proposed truce and startled her. It was probably just as well when her thoughts had turned to flings and relationships at the sight of one sexy smile. This wasn't the time or place, and he certainly wasn't her idea of fun.

'As a producer I'm well versed in getting financial backers on board, so I will definitely see what I can do with regard to your project. I've spoken to the director too and, if you and the other trustees are agreeable, we'd like to film some aspects of the fundraising initiatives going on. Perhaps we could get a sound bite from you on the subject at some point?' Jessica pushed the limits of their newly formed friendship a tad further but she hadn't got where she was today by playing it safe. Besides, they would probably need some lighter moments to balance out a lot of the difficult emotional subject matter. She'd flicked through enough pictures of the volunteers' antics on the website to know they had fun along the fundraising trail, regardless of whatever troubles they had at home or on the ward.

'We'll see.' He didn't commit to doing anything with, or for, her but at least he'd stopped scowling at her. She'd chalk that up as a win.

There was little more Rob could do. He'd made his objections known to the hospital board and the pretty redhead in charge of this madness. From here on in he'd just have to suck it up and put his personal feelings about the media aside.

He'd psyched himself up to do battle this morning over how this circus was going to play out in the department. On the few occasions he'd seen the producer before today she'd been placating the staff with facts and figures on why this would benefit the hospital. The lack of emotion she'd displayed on what was such a heart-rending subject for most people had led Rob to peg her as a cross between a stiff in a trouser suit and another overzealous reporter.

Well, Jessica had blasted the first part of his theory out of the water, bursting in here dressed as if she was going to a wedding. Her wedding. A short white lace dress wasn't the most practical outfit he'd ever seen on the ward. And those shoes—taupe…beige…nude…he wasn't sure of the technical term—he was sure they would send the health and safety lot into a tailspin.

One misstep on those spikes and she'd be heading back out to A&E.

The jury was still out on whether she lived up to his preconceived ideas of media types. It didn't bode well that she already had a list of demands with no thought to the daily running of the place. Unfortunately, cancer didn't work to a timetable and it would be down to her to fit in, not the other way around.

Perhaps he had been hasty in making assumptions about her character but he was extra-sensitive on the subject of privacy. And about intrusive investigators who unwittingly made their subjects' lives hell.

Five years after his wife and daughter had died, he was still trying to come to terms with the car accident and his loss, which had been splashed all over the newspapers. His grief had been compounded by the idea that he'd somehow caused the deaths of his family. If only he hadn't argued with Leah. If only she hadn't stormed out of the house in such a temper because of him. If he'd simply gone with her and Mollie in the first place. Then perhaps they would never have crossed paths with a so-called joyrider. Since the other driver had fled the scene, never to be caught, Rob would never know how events had played out, or ever find closure.

He'd been overwhelmed with so much support from friends and family he'd never been able to tell anyone the truth. That he was to blame and he didn't deserve an ounce of their sympathy. The claustrophobia of his guilt had escalated when the papers had run the story, making him out to be the victim, when he'd known differently. That primal scream had built inside him, ripping him apart in its effort to find release. But he hadn't been able to confess his role when everyone around him was already suffering so much. Instead, he'd taken the easy route and left everyone, everything, back in Scotland.

Of course it wasn't Jessica's fault that he was wary of the press but she'd already proved adept at her research. It wouldn't take much for her to uncover the tragic tale he'd kept secret since taking up his post here. He couldn't bear to have the details raked over again, or stand by and watch anyone else be put in a similar situation for the sake of one woman's career.

Still, she was right about giving the fund some much-needed publicity. As much as it might make him a hypocrite, they were a fair bit away from reaching their two-million-pound target and he would accept any offer of help. No doubt that had played a huge part in getting the families to take part when they were as desperate as he to get a scanner for the department. It would mean quicker diagnosis and treatment, as well as minimising the disruption to the children.

'By requisitioning the storeroom we'll have space for parents and staff to speak freely about certain aspects of the treatment without upsetting anyone around them. Can I pencil you in for a spot?'

Give these investigative types an inch and they took a mile every damn time.

'I have a very busy schedule. Speaking of which, I really need to start my rounds.' He put the first foot forward to escape Jessica's interference and check in with his patients so he could discuss their ongoing care later with the rest of the staff. Unfortunately, his new shadow refused to take the hint and teetered behind him in her high heels.

'I'll put you down as a yes anyway and you can give us a shout when you have a few minutes to spare. Now, the tech crew are set up on the ward, ready to roll. We thought it would be a good idea to film you talking to our little stars. I've already introduced myself but it might make things easier if they see a face they know and trust alongside the cameras.'

Tenacious. That was the word Rob would use to describe her. The most polite one he could think of, at least. It was also how he'd have described his late wife, along with *ambitious*, *stubborn*, *selfish*, *irresponsible* and *terribly missed.*

The argument that fateful day had been over what he'd perceived as neglect of their daughter while she chased her dream. Two adults should've been able to communicate better, discuss arrangements for childcare. Instead of one parent sneaking off to modelling assignments with a bored four-year-old in tow. If he'd handled the situation differently, been aware of his wife's struggle with motherhood earlier...

He dodged away from the dark cloud threatening to settle over him, as it always did when he thought of the accident. The years had done nothing to ease the pain of his loss but there was no room for it here. If these kids were able to wear a brave face through everything they were going through, he could too. After all, they'd done nothing to deserve the hand they'd been dealt and he was guilty of orchestrating his own heartache. He should've been there for his family when they'd needed him most.

'So...we'll make a start, then?' Jessica verbally prodded him.

'Yeah. Sure.' He could at least make preliminary introductions between the patients and the crew. That way he'd be around to make sure Jessica and co. didn't overstep the mark and upset people. He knew better than anyone who was strong enough to bare their soul to the world and who was too fragile to handle the spotlight.

Even with the best will in the world, the sort of attention a personal tragedy brought from the general public could break a person's spirit. There were only so many pitying looks and sympathy one could take before it became too much to bear. But he had the very family in mind who could keep them all on their toes.

'Hey, Max.' As soon as the cameras were ready to roll, Rob perched on the end of his favourite patient's bed, safe in the knowledge that nothing would faze this particular seven-year-old.

'You gonna play cars with me?' Max handed him a red pickup truck from the impressive collection of toy vehicles he had covering the surface of his bed.

'I'm not staying long this morning. I have to show this lady around the ward, but I'll come back later on to see you.' In private.

The demolition derby going on in the centre of the bed came to an abrupt end. 'She's gonna put me on TV.'

'Yes. If that's what you want.' Rob waited for the first indication that this was too much even for his resident funny man.

'Wait!' Max held his hand up to halt everything and Rob heard the collective gasp of the crew as they held their breath.

'Is everything all right?' All he had to do was give the word and this would end now.

'We can stop for a while if that's what you need, Max.' Jessica cut across Rob's concern with the practical solution of a timeout. Clearly she was used to being the one in charge. So was he.

The monitors were still holding steady as they charted the child's vitals, indicating that this wasn't a physiological problem. Max shuffled up the bed and sat straighter.

'I just want to make sure my hair is okay for the cam-

eras. Us TV stars have to look good for the laydees.'
He slid a hand over his little bald head, then slicked a
finger over his non-existent eyebrows.

'Maximus—' Rob tried to hide his own smile whilst
warning his tiny gladiator about making outsiders feel
uncomfortable. Max was too busy rolling on the bed
laughing at his own joke to take any notice. A sense of
humour was an important part of recovery but sometimes the dark nature of it could take others by surprise.

He half expected to see the efficient producer wide-
eyed with horror at one of the chemotherapy-based jokes
which flew about here on a daily basis between the kids.
Instead, those green-blue eyes were sparkling and her
pretty pink lips were curved up into a grin.

'Don't worry—you'll have all the girls falling over
themselves to get to you, Max. Perhaps you'd like to say
a few words to your future fans?' She wasn't the hard-
ass he'd taken her for as she played along, regardless of
the tight schedule she was probably on too.

With the air of a true pro, Rob's charge stopped
laughing and looked directly into the camera lens. 'Hi,
I'm Max. I'm seven and I like cars and strawberry milkshakes.'

'Excellent. Although I'm more partial to chocolate
ones myself.' Jessica wasn't appearing on camera herself but she certainly knew how to get the best from
her subjects. She even had good taste in milkshakes.

'Do you wanna see my central line?' Max pulled
down the front of his hospital gown to show off the long
thin tube inserted into his chest used to administer his
chemotherapy. He was so matter-of-fact about it there
was no room for sympathy or shock. As far as a lot of
the children here were concerned, they were sick and
this was how they got better. It was as simple as that.

The adults, on the other hand, had a much harder time of dealing with it. Max's parents were at his bedside now, happy to let him play up to the cameras, but it had been a long and tearful journey to get this far.

'Wow. That's cool. And can you tell me what it's for?' Jessica gently coaxed some more information from her subject. Since Max and his family seemed relaxed with the line of questioning, Rob would stay out of the conversation unless his counsel was needed.

'The nurses put the medicine in there and sometimes they take blood too.' The plastic tube apparently held no more fear for him than the toys scattered around him, even though he'd suffered some of the awful side effects from the chemo itself. Rob supposed this was simply part of life for the boy now, as it had become for so many of his patients. It was a scenario no parent wanted for their child but it was better than the alternative. He should know. If he'd had the chance, he would've done whatever it took to prolong his own daughter's life. That was part of the process he doubted these new visitors could ever really understand.

'You're a very brave boy, Max. Perhaps Dr Campbell could tell us some more about your condition?' Jessica directed the camera back to him.

Take a deep breath and think of the scanner.

He glanced over at Mr and Mrs Gardner in case they wanted to have their say first.

'I'm going to interview other family members later. For now, I'd appreciate your professional input.' There was no chance of dodging airtime with this eagle-eyed producer on the case. She had all the bases covered and all exits firmly blocked. Rob was back in the spotlight whether he liked it or not.

He cleared his throat. 'Max has Ewing's sarcoma of

the right tibia. This is a rare form of bone cancer usually found in older adolescent males. You're just one in a million, buddy, aren't you?'

Max high-fived him. 'You better believe it.'

'He's responded well to the chemotherapy and is scheduled for surgery to remove the remainder of the tumour.' Rob was savvy enough to understand that Max's surgery was probably another reason he would be top of the producer's wish list, along with his vivacious personality. The drama would be catnip to producers and viewers alike. Rob hoped it would have the happy ending they were all hoping for—complete removal of the tumour and preserving the limb without loss of function. Even then there were no guarantees the cancer wouldn't return or they'd face an eventual amputation down the line. Fortunately, this job was all about taking one step at a time and so far Max's treatment was on target.

'And that's under the guidance of a multidisciplinary team?' Jessica's stealthy research skills again made Rob wonder if they'd yet extended to his personal life.

That familiar churning started in the pit of his stomach, the way it always did when there was a chance he'd have to talk about what had happened with Leah and Mollie. There was no way he was going to be subjected to her questioning or, worse, her pity. 'Yes, Max's care plan has been tailor-made for him under the supervision of the surgeons, nurses, pharmacists and all the other health professionals involved in his treatment thus far.'

He shifted off the bed, not giving a damn if it upset camera angles or continuity; they could always edit. As far as this nonsense was concerned, he'd done what was required of him. More importantly, he'd checked Max wasn't anxious before heading for surgery. 'If you have any other questions, Maria, the senior nurse, can advise you. I really must get on with my rounds.'

Rob was counting on chatterbox Max to keep the crew busy until he'd seen the rest of his patients in peace.

'But…but…' Jessica was tempted to knock him back down on his butt and let her finish this segment. For some reason Dr Campbell seemed intent on sabotaging her at every turn. Just when she thought he was finally coming to terms with their presence here he'd closed up shop again. She was beginning to take it personally when he'd been such a sweetheart to Max.

Rob had switched the minute she'd opened her mouth about the MDT. Perhaps he was territorial and didn't appreciate anyone questioning his methods here. The truth was, she'd spent so long in and out of the oncology ward herself she was practically an expert in the procedures.

It had taken her a while to get used to seeing all the little kids attached to monitors and drips again and she'd actually welcomed having him to lead her through the ward. Sure, she had her hand-picked tech guys here but she was supposed to be the leader as far as they were concerned. There was such a strong association for her with pain and sickness she'd forgotten that there had been good times too. Max had reminded her that she'd had laughs with some real friends along the way. A few of whom hadn't made it out the other side of cancer. Rob had absolutely no cause to treat her as some sort of ghoul.

'Max, I'll come down later and walk with you to Theatre.'

Why couldn't he talk to her with the soft-talking Scottish lilt instead of that defensive bark?

'And maybe we could get that interview on tape while you're here too?' For now she could fire ahead with Max and his parents, but if she couldn't even nail him down for five minutes it was going to be a long couple of months.

'We'll see.' His eyes flashed with blue fire but this wasn't about him, or even her.

'Dr Campbell is one of my best friends. He brings me new cars every time I have to stay here.' Max said his piece on the subject, then resumed making explosion sounds as he caused a four-car pile-up on his bed.

It was a heart-warming statement that managed to smooth out the frown on the handsome doctor's forehead. 'You don't need to suck up, Max. We both know I have a silver Lamborghini with your name on it.'

These two together were cuteness personified. Jessica understood that the staff developed close bonds with the children—she'd become attached to the nurses she'd seen nearly every day—but it was rare for someone of Rob's status to take such a personal interest. He would probably relate more if he had boys of his own but Jessica knew nothing of his personal circumstances.

He turned his back on her to walk away but that terrier spirit in her wanted his name in her diary before he left. She reached out to stop him. 'So, we can go ahead and schedule that interview?'

The muscles in his arm bunched beneath her fingers and she had to fight to concentrate. This was a guy who worked out and someone she clearly had explosive chemistry with. Unfortunately, a quick check on his ring finger confirmed he was already taken.

'Why do I get the impression that not many people say no to you?' Rob cocked his head to one side as though he was studying some new incurable disease.

Goosebumps rippled over her skin. In her job she was used to being challenged; the thrill of it reminded her she was alive. Although, judging by her quickening pulse, it could be said she was enjoying it too much at present.

'They do. I simply choose to ignore it.' Something she was going to have to do about those hottie vibes radiating from her new *married* opponent.

CHAPTER TWO

Rob switched on the air conditioning in his car in an attempt to cool the after-effects of his early-morning workout and hot shower. He reckoned the gym was missing a trick with their opening times. A twenty-four-hour haven for members whose shift patterns and insomnia left them with too much time on their hands would make a fortune.

He'd stayed at the hospital until after Max's surgery, making sure there was a friendly face by his side when he came round from the anaesthetic. Even though he'd been exhausted by the time he'd returned home and fallen into bed, the tiredness hadn't overridden the all too familiar nightmares. Rob might not have been at the scene of the accident but it didn't stop him imagining their terror, hearing them call for him before the sickening crunch of the impact.

Sometimes he would even wake from his fitful sleep thinking he could hear Mollie crying from the room next door, a sound which always pulled on his heartstrings like a harp. He'd be out of bed and on his way to tuck her in before he realised his mind had played a cruel trick on him. Thanks to his own stubbornness and a dumb kid in a stolen car, he'd never have a chance to comfort his daughter again.

The first rays of the dawn light often came as a blessing, heralding the start of a new working day where he had plenty to keep his thoughts busy. It was the downtime, such as sitting in this logjam of cars, which let his mind wander towards those things beyond his control.

As he edged forward in the morning traffic, he spotted a familiar figure by the side of the road. Jessica, with her slinky grey silk dress hitched up to her thighs, was running after a bus, barefoot. Rob slowed the car to watch the spectacle. Sure enough, there she was with those ludicrous heels in her hand for a second time. Silver ones today. He wouldn't be surprised if she had matching shoes for every outfit in her, no doubt, vast wardrobe.

He wound down the window as he tailed her. 'You should really invest in a pair of flats.'

She slowed to a casual walk although her face was flushed from her exertions and he'd already heard her swear as the bus pulled away. Jessica leaned through the open window and the auburn waves of her hair tumbled over her shoulders. 'Are you going to sit there sneering all day, or be a gentleman and offer me a lift?'

He opened the door and turned off his MP3 player so he didn't lose the upper hand here by revealing his love of cheesy pop music. Even though she was the last person he wanted to spend time with, he could hardly leave her stranded when they were going to the same place. Next time he might be inclined to pretend he didn't see her and save himself from suffocating in her spicy perfume.

'I didn't have you down as the type to use public transport,' he remarked.

The expensive clothes and the matching pearly-pink mani-pedi she was sporting weren't in keeping with the thick exhaust fumes belching out from the bus in front. No, she'd be more at home in a sports car with the top down, cruising the streets of Monaco or somewhere equally fabulous.

'I never did get around to taking driving lessons. Besides, the buses run regularly into the city centre from here and I don't have to worry about finding a parking space. It's my fault I'm late. I slept in this morning.' Jessica leaned one hand on his leg to balance herself as she bent down to slip on her shoes. It was such an innocent, yet intimate, act but it burned his skin where she touched him. The rush of blood in his ears drowned out the majority of her chatter—something about missing breakfast—as she squeezed his thigh.

He hadn't expected to react so...primitively...to being in close quarters with a woman he'd barely spoken to until twenty-four hours ago. It wasn't as if he'd been a monk all of this time, where one touch from a woman could send him into raptures. He'd had a few flings but he lived by three rules—no one from work, no more than one night and keep things strictly physical. His partners knew the score from the start, so he could walk away without any emotional complications. No one would ever get close enough where he'd have to battle his conscience over replacing Leah in his life.

Jessica was attractive, successful and apparently incredibly tactile. What wasn't to like? Unless you only engaged in overnight shenanigans and the lady in question was at your place of work for the next four weeks. In other circumstances he might have acted differently, encouraged further exploration of his person, but this would only be asking for trouble. He shuffled in his seat as his body seemed to outgrow his trousers and he was glad when she removed her hand before things became uncomfortable for both of them.

'I…er…thought you might like to know Max's surgery was a success. The surgeon managed to remove all traces of the tumour.' He switched back to the topic guaranteed to draw out her ruthless side and remind him she was a no-go area.

'I already know, but thanks.'

'Oh, I wasn't aware you were still filming him?' He hadn't seen any cameras down near the operating theatre and it wasn't the sort of information the staff would've given her over the phone.

'We weren't. I got a text from his mum, Maggie, last night. I keep in touch with most of the parents to see how the kids are doing. Not everyone thinks I'm the devil incarnate.' She was trying to get a rise out of him but she'd managed that with one snippet of information.

He couldn't believe she was close enough to the families that they included her in their circle of trust. If what she was saying was true, that information on the children's health wasn't even gleaned for the benefit of the show. He would have to rethink what he thought he knew about her. His jaded perception of anyone in the media world had meant that he'd thought it impossible for her to be genuinely invested in these kids. To find out otherwise meant he might have to actually start being nice to her. At work.

'Well, I'm pleased you have such a personal interest in the families but I hope you understand we still can't have you breezing in and out as you please. We're not going to hold back treatment to fit in around your schedule.' The deliberately harsh words were an attempt to establish boundaries in a situation where he was scrabbling for an ounce of control. She was a member of staff by proxy and privileged to have been given access to the ward, after all.

'I assure you I'm deadly serious about this job. My timekeeping is usually impeccable. Unfortunately, I didn't sleep very well last night and didn't hear the alarm go off this morning. I'm sure even you've over-slept on occasion but you have my word it won't hap-pen again.' Jessica stiffened in the passenger seat, her hands resting very properly in her lap as she rose above his accusation of complacency.

'Good.' Rob jammed the car into fifth gear as they got a free run onto the motorway.

'Fine.'

An uneasy silence filled the interior of the car as they retreated back to their corners. Rob might have successfully asserted his authority over the crew's pres-ence in the department, but he'd also ploughed up any groundwork they'd laid for a semi-harmonious working relationship. All because he couldn't handle being this close to another woman without freaking out about it.

'Isn't there someone else who could give you a nudge in the mornings, or give you a lift into work?' He didn't know why he was pushing for more information about her home life. Whether she had a partner or still lived at home with her parents was of no consequence to him. Perhaps he was simply hoping there was someone else in her life to take responsibility for getting her to work on time so he didn't have to.

'I'm single and rediscovering the joys of indepen-dence. How about you?' There spoke the voice of a bitter break-upee. Someone who probably wasn't in a hurry to jump back into a relationship of any sort. Not that her love life was of any consequence to him.

He had no desire to get involved in the details of her

split, nor did he want to get caught up in an exchange of personal information with a virtual stranger. After a moment he decided to go with 'Unhappily single' to describe his current status. He wasn't alone by choice, and he wasn't too fond of the other label usually bestowed on him, since it portrayed him as some sort of tragic case.

'What, no Mrs Campbell to see you off to work in the morning with a kiss and some freshly cut sandwiches?' The sneer in Jessica's voice declared her judgement on the sort of woman she imagined married to him. How little she knew. Leah's free-spirited nature hadn't been dampened simply because she'd become a wife and mother. If anything, Rob had been the one in the relationship more suited to domesticity. Not that he would admit that to a woman who'd already challenged his authority and coerced him into making concessions for her benefit. A woman not unlike the one he'd lost.

'Not any more.' He tightened his grip on the steering wheel, trying to strangle the emotions bubbling up inside him, and put his foot down on the accelerator to get to the hospital as soon as possible. Post shift was the time for wallowing in his grief, certainly not before. It wouldn't do to cross his personal life with his professional one or he'd end up a complete blubbering mess every time a family reminded him of his. And what purpose would he have in life if he couldn't even do his job properly?

'Did she forget to cut your crusts off once too often?' The throwaway remark came with a snort but the subject was too raw for Rob to find any amusement.

'She died.' He didn't have to turn his head to know

he'd left Jessica open-mouthed; those words always had the same effect when he was forced to say them.

Usually he resisted telling people about his personal circumstances for as long as he could. This time, instead of reliving the horror by bringing it up, he found some relief in sharing his secret. It was somehow less painful than he'd imagined. In that brief moment he'd been able to actually be himself and stop pretending he was a man who had it all. As if he'd exhaled the toxins of the past in one deep, cleansing breath.

It was something he should've confided a long time ago. He knew Maria and plenty of others were curious about his wedding ring and lack of wife but he'd never been drawn to spill the details. It would only have led to more questions he wasn't prepared to answer.

There was something he recognised of himself in Jessica. Something about her which put him at ease in her company. Something dangerous.

'I'm sorry.' Jessica mentally facepalmed as she suffered a bout of foot-in-mouth disease. She would never have made such crass comments if she'd known he was a widower. In truth, she'd only said those things to remind herself that he was out of bounds. Her libido had pinged back to full strength when she'd felt those strong muscular thighs beneath her fingers. Now here she was having hot flashes which were more to do with lusting over a grieving man than her hormones. Mother Nature's timing was as atrocious as ever.

'Thanks.' Rob kept his eyes firmly on the road, leaving Jessica unable to read him. His locked-out arms and firmly set jaw told her she probably wasn't meant to, but it would be remiss of her not to probe further when he'd volunteered that first revealing nugget.

'Was your wife Scottish too, or local?' It was a question Jessica deemed not too intrusive but designed to give her an idea of the timeline involved here. He was still wearing his wedding ring after all. Rob had been at the hospital for a few years, so if he'd met his other half after he'd started his post here it could have been a recent passing. Even Jessica wouldn't put a newly bereaved doctor in front of the camera if he still had issues to work through. She made a note to quiz Maria Dean, the senior nurse on staff, who, unlike Rob, always seemed happy to talk.

'Leah was from Edinburgh, same as me.' The muscle in Rob's jaw twitched and Jessica could almost hear his teeth grinding together.

A name. An indication that he'd probably come to Northern Ireland after her death. Progress.

'Do you mind me asking—'

'Can we drop this, please?' This time he did look at her, shooting blue laser beams at her and leaving her under no illusion that the subject was a no-go zone for the foreseeable future. Apparently he did mind, cutting her off before she could enquire about what had happened to Leah.

'Sure. Sorry.' She was. Sorry she'd got him offside again, sorry he'd lost his wife and, most of all, sorry she'd brought it all back to him.

They spent the rest of the car journey to work in silence, Rob clearly lost in his memories and Jessica unwilling to say anything more in case she upset him further. If circumstances were reversed, she wouldn't appreciate anyone prying into her past to open old wounds either. Although her ex was still very much alive, it didn't make reminders of him any less painful.

Each time Adam came to mind, he brought thoughts of her own failings with him.

Perhaps Rob was going through something similar, taking the blame for events most probably beyond his control. She'd only recently begun working free of that guilt trap herself. That was why this job meant so much to her. Although she'd ultimately flunked the wife exam, she could still be a success in other areas of her life. It had taken a long time for her to come to terms with that.

It was possible she'd found a kindred spirit who'd also channelled all of his energy into his career rather than risk the heartache of another relationship. The thought comforted her even though the renewed awkwardness between them was palpable, since Rob didn't seem inclined to even switch the radio on. Jessica didn't dare defy him any further by doing it herself.

The heavy atmosphere in the car only began to lift when the familiar glass building came into sight. Most likely he was as eager to get to work as she was and check his personal baggage at the hospital door. There was nothing like deadlines and adrenaline to clear the head first thing in the morning.

Jessica unclipped her seat belt and reached for the door handle. 'Thanks for the lift. I'll jump out here.'

While Rob waited for the barrier to open at the entrance to the staff car park, Jessica made a swift exit from the vehicle to give him some time out. Maybe if he had some space from her for a few minutes he could forget she'd done the one thing she'd promised not to do. *Privacy* was his keyword and she'd tried to swerve his to satisfy her own agenda. Since he was the lead here it was going to take an extra effort to convince him she wasn't Satan's daughter recording peoples' suffering for kicks. He was the first man since Adam whom she wanted to know there was a soft heart beneath her crisp, ruthless producer shell.

'Did I see you arrive with Jessica this morning?' Maria interrupted Rob's thoughts as he flicked through his schedule for the day.

'My good deed for the day. Don't read anything into it.' He warned her off before she started her match-making mischief again. Ever since coming here he'd had to endure her futile attempts to see him settled down again.

He was sure Maria meant well but he needed a break from awkward dinner dates and disappointment. He didn't *want* to forget. Grief, Leah and Mollie were all part of him. He didn't want to move on and pretend that the best and worst things in his life had never happened. His wife and daughter deserved to be remembered and he deserved to live with the guilt of what had happened for the rest of his life.

Luckily for Maria, he could never get cross with her when she'd been his lifeline in a sea of despair. They'd immediately bonded over their shared devotion to their patients when he'd first started here. He hadn't told her, or any of his colleagues, about the accident even though it was clear he was on his own. He didn't want anyone to see him as anything other than a leader of his field. It was in everyone's best interests that he remained the strong stalwart during the hardships they faced here and not simply another grieving parent. Although it didn't stop her from setting him up with the nearest available spinster at every given opportunity.

'Why not? She's young, single, attractive...'

And definitely not the settling-down type. The ideal

woman for a no-emotions-required fling if they were both looking for one. There was just something about Jessica Halliday that set Rob's Spidey senses on high alert.

'I don't dispute the facts but you forgot to mention *nosy* and *incredibly frustrating*.' He'd known her only five minutes and she'd already unearthed more about his personal life than most of his colleagues were privy to. He wasn't in a hurry to share any more.

'Ah, she's got under your skin already.' Maria nodded with a knowing Rob-baiting smile.

'Not at all.' She was most definitely under his skin, to the point of irritation, but he didn't want Maria encouraging Jessica's interest, or vice versa. The last thing he needed was another concerned female hell-bent on getting him to dig deep into his emotion bank. That sucker was closed tight, hermetically sealed, weighted down and buried at the bottom of the River Lagan.

'I had several meetings with her in the lead-up to filming. She's no wallflower, that's for sure. Definitely not afraid to voice her opinion or ask difficult questions. Is that what you're afraid of?' Maria cocked an eyebrow at him. She knew him too well.

'I'm not averse to a strong-minded woman, as you very well know.' He gave her a flirty wink and hoped it was enough to end the conversation.

Instead, Maria rested her hand gently on top of Rob's in that sympathetic way that always made him want to push her away. He'd moved to Belfast to escape the pity party, not find himself as the guest of honour at another one. 'Don't give up on love. The right person is out there for you somewhere.'

Every time Rob heard those words he imagined a saxophone and some electric guitar playing him his very own power ballad. All he needed was a fog machine and a mullet and he'd be the epitome of eighties angst. He'd had the right person and she was gone. Nothing could change that.

Lucky for him he was in a busy hospital ward and not the dingy bedroom of his teenage self, so there was nowhere for him to sit and wail over the girl he'd lost.

Jessica's head was pounding and her stomach begging for something more substantial than the two headache tablets she'd consumed. She'd missed breakfast this morning and ended up skipping lunch in favour of a particularly fraught meeting with the director over content. He wanted more footage of Rob outside of his hospital role so that viewers were able to relate to him on a personal level as well as a professional one. That was akin to asking her to produce footage of the Loch Ness monster.

On top of that, she wasn't relishing the turn today's filming was about to take. It was going to be a tough one for all involved. She'd spoken to the family concerned to ensure they were ready to tell their daughter Lauren's story on camera and she was aware there would be no happy ending to this tale. Unfortunately, palliative care was part of cancer and it didn't discriminate against age. The treatment might help to make the patient more comfortable in the short-term but it wouldn't cure the illness.

Jessica didn't have to have children of her own to understand how incredibly distressing this would be. The professional producer in her agreed with the director that they had to include light and shade if they were going to chart the reality of the department. Her heart, however, wanted her to avoid any further reminder of cancer's destructive nature. This was a child, a baby, who'd been denied a second chance at life. In the end, it was the family who'd made the final decision to go ahead. They were keen to highlight Lauren's condition in the hope that a cure would be found some day. Jessica would simply have to try to remain emotionally detached from the subject. Easier said than done.

She massaged her temples as that heavy pressure seemed to bore down further inside her skull. The smell of coffee and cake hit her as she walked through the entrance hall on her way to meet the camera crew and she saw a few of the parents had set up a stall in the main foyer selling tray bakes and goodies to add to the scanner coffers. There were several tables and chairs dotted around for visitors and staff to take a timeout along with their treats.

Rob was there, talking and laughing with the mums with a box full of home-baked goodies in his hands. He really went above and beyond the call of duty for his patients and their families. The TV business wasn't exactly a breeding ground for that kind of altruism and Jessica found it refreshing. It was a pity she'd been such a cow to him this morning by prying into his private life. He was a nice guy and it had been a long time since she'd met one of those.

She started towards the stall to offer an apology and try to make amends but her legs wobbled beneath her. A heaviness settled over her entire body and she was helpless as she felt herself falling. Rob rushing towards her was the last thing she saw before darkness claimed her.

'Jessica?'

Lost in the swirling fog, Jessica could hear someone in the distance calling her name.

'Jessica?'

She wasn't ready to leave her peaceful slumber and cuddled further into the warmth surrounding her.

'Can you open your eyes for me, sweetheart?'

Jessica frowned. 'Go away.'

'I will as soon as we get you back on your feet.'

'What?' In her fugue state she swore she could hear Rob whispering in her ear to bring her body back to life.

'You fainted.'

Her eyes slowly fluttered open to find her dream date only a breath away. She didn't know what she was doing in his arms but she kind of liked it. His hard chest was pressed tight against her, his large hands splayed across her back so she was cocooned in his spicy musk and muscles.

'Can you stand on your own?'

Jessica blinked again and tried to focus. It soon became clear that their passionate embrace was more of a clumsy tango as Rob fought to keep her dropping to the floor like a sack of spuds.

'I'm so sorry. I don't know what happened.' She pushed against him to free herself from his hold and the embarrassing scene she'd created. The feel of his rounded biceps under her fingertips did nothing to help her equilibrium.

'Let's get you into a seat.' He lessened his grip but stayed with her until he'd deposited her into a chair at the makeshift café.

'I'm fine,' she insisted even though her head was still spinning. She hated showing any weakness, especially if it meant relying on a man to rescue her. Until now she'd been standing on her own two feet for some considerable time.

'I want you to put your head between your legs and take some deep breaths.'

She only complied since he was the doctor and she was apparently having difficulty staying conscious.

Rob rubbed her back as she inhaled. 'Do you feel dizzy?'

'A bit.' Another big breath in and his hand rose and fell with her.

'When was the last time you had something to eat? I know you missed breakfast and I doubt you've sat still long enough for a proper lunch break, have you?'

'Um…I had a cup of coffee this morning and some headache tablets. I've been busy with other things…'

'That explains it. You can't survive on a diet of coffee and adrenaline, you know. I understand your need to direct all of your energy into your work but it's important to stop and refuel every now and then.'

'Yes, Doctor.'

'You need something to raise your blood sugar and you definitely need to give yourself a break from these.' He crouched down in front of her and cradled her foot in his hands as the Cinderella scene played out in reverse.

Thanks to his open top button, Jessica had a nice view down the front of Rob's shirt. The smooth swarthy skin beneath contrasting against his crisp white shirt was not the usual skin tone of a fair-skinned native. Her feverish mind began to conjure up images of her handsome prince soaking up the rays in a lot less than a tailored shirt and formal black trousers.

She didn't do romance but she imagined it probably looked a lot like a burly doctor on his knees gently removing a girl's stilettos. He sat back on his haunches to face her again and reached up to brush the curls from her face. Her whole body tensed as if she was waiting for that one magical kiss that followed the princess's rescue at the end of every fairy tale.

One of the stallholders interrupted the tender moment to hand Prince Charming a glass of water, her eyes darting between Jessica and Rob as she clearly jumped to conclusions.

He thanked her and proceeded to tangle his free hand in Jessica's hair again.

'What are you doing?' She sprang back in her chair, now fully conscious and aware they weren't alone in the busy thoroughfare. Goodness knew what people were making of this whole episode but it probably wasn't anything which would improve her credibility here.

'You have cream in your hair.' Rob plucked at another strand to produce chocolatey proof that he wasn't randomly stroking her hair.

'*Oh.* Why?' This day was getting better and better.

'You squashed my buns,' he said with a grin and nodded towards the spot where she'd made her dramatic entrance.

Now cordoned off with safety cones, the area resembled something of a crime scene as efficient cleaners swept away the aftermath of an apparent cake massacre. The broken remains of cupcakes and caramel squares lay in a pool of cream and sprinkles on the floor.

'I can't believe you sacrificed cake for me. The actions of a true hero.' She clutched her hands to her chest in exaggerated appreciation, attempting to deflect attention away from the effect his touch had had on her. The hairs on her arms were still standing on end where he'd made physical contact. Obviously, in all the confusion her body had mistaken him for a potential mate. Her mind was having a harder time dealing with the idea when he represented everything that made her feel weak.

Sitting here, helpless and dependent on his instruction, took her back to a time when every decision about how she lived her life was taken out of her hands by doctors. Rationally, she knew it had all been in her best interests but she'd spent too long fighting for independence to relinquish it so easily now. Even to a doctor who could easily have made it as Mr June in the *Hunks* calendar currently hanging on her apartment wall.

'What else is a man to do when a beautiful woman swoons at his feet?' Rob moved to a standing position so Jessica was forced to strain her neck looking up at him. She ignored the tiny voice in her head squealing at the inadvertent compliment he'd paid her since the conversation between them had turned jovial.

Given their run-ins to date, Jessica doubted she was his type in any shape or form. Rob Campbell was destined to be part of a couple; her fate lay in a completely different direction. There was no point in even thinking there was any kind of entanglement on the cards. So she should really stop wondering if he had any hidden tan lines.

'I hate to burst your bubble but, as you said, it was probably from lack of food rather than a reaction to your good looks.' Jessica couldn't believe she'd actually fainted. She supposed she was burning off more calories than usual with all this toing and froing. In future, she'd keep a few snacks to hand to fend off further embarrassment.

'I can offer you some sweet tea and a cupcake for now but I'd advise you to eat a proper lunch as soon as you can.' He left her and took his place in the queue to purchase her temporary cure.

He wanted the best for everyone he treated, her included. At least this mishap had softened his attitude towards her. Even if it had come at the price of her dignity. Rob was sympathetic, passionate, dedicated...

everything a woman would want in a long-term partner. It was just as well Jessica didn't want one or she
would be in real danger of falling for him.

CHAPTER THREE

JESSICA NIBBLED AT the slice of chocolate fudge cake and sipped the sweet tea Rob had provided until she started to feel like herself again. The fear of falling into a sugar coma prevented her from finishing it all. Rob had no such qualms and tossed his empty paper plate and cup into the bin.

'All better?'

'Yes. Thank you. I should head on over to the ward. I don't want to keep the O'Neills waiting.' This job didn't make allowances for illness or time off for busy producers who forgot to eat. She was responsible for everything that happened in front of, and behind, the screens. The success of the programme ultimately rested on her shoulders and she sure as hell wouldn't let a hunger-induced dizzy spell hold her back.

The next step on the career ladder was Executive Producer, where she could lead her own production from concept to completion. She wanted the responsibility for selecting and marketing a range of TV shows including dramas and documentaries.

'Ah, yes. They said you were doing a piece on them. I'll walk over with you.'

'There's no need. I promise we'll be respectful and sympathetic at all times.' Her hackles rose at the assumption she couldn't be sensitive, Jessica got up from her chair ready to march away. Only, the cold tiled floor beneath her bare feet reminded her she had to put her shoes back on before she could do that with any dignity.

'I'm glad to hear it. However, it's you I'm thinking about.'

Jessica's pulse beat a little faster and sent her head spinning again as Rob fixed her under that intense gaze of his. She knew he meant that he was concerned about her fainting spell but there was something inherently sexy in hearing those words. Especially when they were delivered in a spine-tingling Scottish rumble from a handsome doctor.

'Honestly, there's no need.' She was so used to fighting her own battles she'd forgotten what it was like to have someone watch her back. It probably wouldn't do her any good to get used to the idea when she was here only for a matter of weeks.

She wedged her shoes back on her feet so she was no longer at a disadvantage standing next to him. It wasn't as if she was some delicate creature who needed a man to make her feel safe. Not any more.

'I don't want to be held responsible for you swooning into the arms of another unsuspecting man.' He moved aside to let her pass.

'That was a one-off. Although I could be tempted to do it more often if it means I get force-fed chocolate cake every time.' She kept quiet about the bigger perk of having him hold her close, since it completely obliterated her ice queen image.

'That's not a bad plan. I might use it myself. Seriously, though, you should be taking it easy.'

Jessica opened her mouth to protest but Rob held his hands up and stopped her.

'I know, I know. That's never going to happen. Hence the personal escort. Shall we?'

He was being so courteous that Jessica wouldn't have been surprised if he'd offered her his arm like some nineteenth-century gent taking her courting. It left her no option but to let him accompany her.

If she was honest, as they stepped back onto the ward, she was glad to have his support for the next leg of her journey.

'Can you tell us something about Lauren's background? It would help the audience to understand the situation now.' Jessica's mouth was dry, her heart heavy as she addressed Mr and Mrs O'Neill at the bedside.

She admired their strength for wanting to share their story during what was probably the worst time of their lives. Their total devotion to their child made Jessica think of what her own parents had gone through. She'd always focused on how the cancer treatment had affected *her* but they must have gone through hell too. They weren't to know their only child would make it past the hair loss and sickness into adulthood. A comfort also denied to the O'Neill family.

'Lauren was first diagnosed with a brain tumour just after her second birthday. She had major surgery, followed by radiotherapy and chemotherapy.' Mrs O'Neill carried on stroking her daughter's hand whilst she was talking. Lauren was smiling up at her even though she was clearly very weak and the love they had for each other was tangible.

Despite the tragic circumstances, Jessica still had a pang to experience that mother/daughter bond from the other side of the equation. She knew how it felt to *be* loved by a parent but she could only imagine the strength of that love *for* a child. That was part of a relationship she would never get to experience and never fully understand.

A hush descended over the private room and Jessica sensed that they were all hesitant to go further into the details of Lauren's illness. There had been a purposeful attempt to make the hospital room as cheerful as possible with get-well-soon cards papering the walls and brightly coloured balloons and toys stuffed into every available space. It was difficult to be the one who had to make them face the reality of what the future held.

Jessica swallowed hard before she tried to coax some more information from the family. 'Can you tell me what happened after the initial treatment?'

The last thing she expected was to see Mr and Mrs O'Neill smiling as they were asked to cast their minds back to those days. Even Rob stopped looking so pained at the intrusion into his patient's business.

'They removed the tumour entirely and Lauren recovered well. We had sixteen fabulous cancer-free months catching up on all of the fun things we'd missed out on during the chemo. You loved the zoo, didn't you, sweetheart?' Lauren's mum was tenderly stroking her head as she recounted the happy memories.

'I liked the monkeys best.' Lauren's small croaky voice was so full of childish wonder it broke Jessica's heart. There was so much of life she would never get to experience.

Despite her residual health problems, Jessica was reminded how incredibly lucky she was.

'Yes, and Daddy bought you one, didn't he?' Mrs

O'Neill reached for the long-armed pink primate hanging from the corner of the bed and handed it to her daughter. Lauren cuddled into her treasured souvenir of the day with a smile.

'Does he have a name, Lauren?' Jessica was almost too choked up to ask.

'Pinky.' The unimaginative name from the four-year-old brought some nervous laughter from the assembled group.

'Lauren started to get sick again shortly after that day. The cancer had come back. To her spine this time. We'd already been told if it came back—' Mrs O'Neill's voice caught on a sob. She didn't have to finish the sentence for Jessica to understand there would be no cure.

Jessica had first-hand experience of the cruelty of false hope. Six months into her own remission she'd suffered a relapse. That period of respite where she'd been able to live like any other eleven-year-old girl had been brief. Birthday parties and girlie afternoons with her friends had been replaced once more with hospital appointments and sickness. Even now that fear of a decline in her health still shadowed her.

'Lauren's been having treatment to try to make her more comfortable so she can go home. We'll take another scan in a few weeks' time to see if the chemo has slowed the growth of the tumour.' Rob stepped in when it seemed Mrs O'Neill couldn't continue. Essentially, he was saying there was nothing more they could do for Lauren except make her last days more bearable and give her some quality time with her family.

Jessica didn't know how he managed to deal with this every day and still function as well as he did. Most of the time she was able to compartmentalise her life in a similar way. It was either file away this kind of trauma and get on with your own life or bawl your eyes out and eat your own body weight in chocolate. But it took a certain level of detachment not to be affected by the helpless babe, hooked up to bleeping machines and monitors, that even a hard-hearted producer didn't have.

She brought a halt to filming, not wishing to prolong the family's agony. Any further commentary could be added in the edits when she'd distanced herself from events. For now, watching these people whispering endearments to their innocent daughter as her life ebbed away was too much. It was intrusive and everything else Rob had said it would be. She wouldn't air anything they might later come to regret committing to tape.

'Thank you so much for letting us speak to you today. And, Lauren—' She wanted to offer some words of comfort but there would be no getting better, or second chances. All that came out of her mouth was a strangled cry and the tears she'd been desperately trying to hold back teetered on the edge of her eyelashes.

'Jessica will be back later to see you, Lauren. She has to go and finish making your TV programme so she can make you a big star.' Rob brought another smile to the little girl's lips so easily when all Jessica could do was see the sadness.

Two large hands rested on her shoulders and she didn't resist as they steered her away from the bedside and into the corridor. In other circumstances she would've shrugged Rob off and given him a dressing-down for undermining her. On this occasion she had to concede he was right. She wouldn't do anyone any good blubbing by the bedside when those worst affected by the situation were coping so much better than she was. That was the strength of a family, leaning on each other for support to get through the darkest days. Something she would never have for herself.

'I feel so, so sorry for them.' She exited the room in a daze, following Rob along the corridor simply because she didn't know where else to go. As much as she wanted to be able to do something for Lauren, she clearly wasn't in the right frame of mind to be of any use.

'We all do but they need *us* to be strong in order for them to remain strong. If you fall apart, they fall apart. Do you understand?'

Jessica bit her lip and nodded, doing her best to keep it together. She'd seen and heard some truly awful things while working as a journalist in the city centre before moving into TV and always managed to remain professional. It was the combination of such innocence tainted by the very thing which had wrecked her life which rendered her an emotional jellyfish.

'It wasn't my intention to upset them.'

Rob might be more understanding of her intense reaction if he knew her history. Indeed, had *she* been more mindful of how close she was to the subject matter she might have prevented upsetting a lot of people. Herself included.

'I accept that but we try to keep things as upbeat as we can here. We need to focus on the positives and take one day at a time or else we'd all go mad. Lauren's still here and she's not in pain. That's all we can hope for at the minute.'

Jessica hated not being able to do anything to help when she was so used to being in a position of power. Right now, the only thing still under her control was her personal life and she intended to keep a tight hold of the reins on that. Otherwise there was a chance she'd end up as one of life's victims. Again.

'Are you all right?' Rob turned back to check on Jessica, since she hadn't responded to his comment or bombarded him with a hundred questions about the next course of action. Despite her position, she wasn't very adept at hiding her feelings. This was clearly getting to her. He'd heard it in her voice and seen it in her eyes. It wasn't an uncommon reaction to being in the department; he simply hadn't expected it from *her*.

His first impression of her as a ruthless career woman was turning out to be false. From the moment they'd met, Jessica had made it very clear she was all about her work. He'd never expected her to have room for compassion along with her ambition, or let anyone see that side of her.

If anything, here was a woman who wore her heart on the sleeve of her designer dress. The very opposite of him. He went out of his way to disguise his emotions so no one ever came close to reading him. An air of mystery was preferable to people interfering or judging him.

In the space of twenty-four hours, however, he'd already seen Jessica irritated, vulnerable and sad. He found himself looking forward to seeing her happy and excited phases.

'I'm fine.' *I'm fine.* Those two words a woman could say and mean a thousand different things. In the end, though, it always boiled down to two facts. She wasn't fine, and she didn't want to talk about it.

The unusually high-pitched denial and trembling bottom lip told a different story. There was no way she could possibly go back to work in this state and not regret it.

'My office. Now.' Jaw clenched, nostrils flaring, Rob corralled her into a side room. There were some tricks to maintaining that aloof facade and he was willing to give her the benefit of his experience. Something he would do for anyone on staff. A timeout would give her the chance to compose herself before she went back on the floor firing out orders to her underlings. As he'd explained, they couldn't let their personal distress show in the middle of the children's ward.

The minute he'd closed the door behind them, everything Jessica had been holding inside came bubbling to the surface until a torrent of tears were streaming down her face.

'I'm…so…sorry,' she stuttered through her sobs.

'Don't be. You're only human.' Rob lost a piece of his heart to every child who came through those doors too, along with their families. If he was honest, he was glad to see that Jessica was developing an emotional attachment to the kids. It meant they were more to her than purely ratings fodder and that was all he could ask of her.

He took a handkerchief from his pocket to give to her and received a watery smile in return. The sniffing and spluttering started to subside. 'I'm usually not like this.'

'We all have our moments.' He'd shed a tear for every child they'd lost, albeit in private. The ones who reminded him of his own daughter took him a little longer to get over. A vision of his daughter's cute smile, so like her mother's, brought a lump to his throat. He swallowed it down and tried not to think how the nine-year-old version would've turned out. Would she still have been a daddy's girl? Or too embarrassed to be seen with him as she headed into those rebellious teenage years?

Jessica began weeping again and Rob automatically

moved towards her. As a doctor, it wasn't in his nature to ignore someone in distress. As a man, he couldn't stand by and watch a woman crying without doing something about it. Especially when that woman was only releasing the emotions he insisted on keeping locked inside. He envied her ability to express herself so openly.

'Let it all out,' he said as he stepped forward to fold her into his arms.

Moments such as this often made him wonder if the medical staff who'd been on the scene of Leah and Mollie's accident had cried for them. Had anyone offered them comfort?

There was only a slight hesitation before Jessica accepted him as a shoulder to literally cry on, her tears soaking through his shirt. Rob rubbed her back as he consoled her. Perhaps he should have prepared his new colleague more for life on the ward. He'd been too caught up in his own issues about what she did for a living to think about the woman behind the title.

She smelled so good. Like chocolate, tea and spicy perfume, mixed together to create all the comforts of home in one glorious package. For a split second, with Jessica in his arms, he let himself believe he could be part of a couple again, sharing fears and finding comfort in each other. But then what? He'd have to come clean about failing his family. Worse, repeat the same mistake over again and risk destroying more lives.

It was tempting to stay in this bubble and hide from the cruelty of the outside world but he was in serious danger of crossing a line here. Jessica wasn't one of his patients; she wasn't even technically a member of staff. Yet he cared about what she was going through. That didn't fit well with his no-emotional-attachments rule when it came to attractive single women.

'As soon as my shift is over, I'm taking you home.' He could still be sympathetic while creating some distance at the same time.

'Okay.' She sniffed as another wave of sorrow claimed her. It immediately called out to the protector in him which had once lived to serve the women in his life. He'd been there to patch up every cut knee Mollie had, to hold her when she'd cried, and suddenly that had all been ripped away from him.

Rob rested his chin on her head and stroked her hair until the storm subsided.

He missed being needed.

Jessica left the rest of the production team to view the dailies in the gallery while she went for a much-needed caffeine injection. As prescribed by Dr Campbell, she'd eaten a late lunch and intended to leave work at a sensible time. However, neither of those suggestions had managed to lift her spirits, or her energy, after the day from hell. It was unusual for her to be so drained by a shoot and she was going to have to get her head back in the game soon before anyone other than Rob noticed.

She still couldn't believe he'd been there to witness her epic meltdown. Not to mention the whole fainting episode. When the mood took him, Dr Campbell had the perfect bedside manner but her reputation as a no-nonsense ruthless TV exec was seriously in jeopardy. On a personal level, she had to admit it had been nice to have a shoulder to cry on. Despite having now earned her empowered women membership badge, Jessica had enjoyed having someone to stroke her hair and tell her everything would be all right. It was a shame it was nothing more than a fantasy. She would never rely on a man for any longer than those few minutes of madness today. It was the only way to keep her heart safe.

Jessica made her way to the vending machines by the hospital entrance, since the main catering was a bit of a hike away for someone balancing her entire body weight on the spikes of her stilettos. She was lost in thought watching the dark liquid fill the paper cup and wondering how bad it would taste when she felt a hand at her waist.

'Are you ready to go?' Rob's low voice in her ear sent a jolt right through her entire body, doing more to re-invigorate her than the iffy-looking coffee ever could.

She thought seriously about telling him to go without her. The snot crying and snuggling had been so out of character for her, she was tempted to walk home in the rain before letting him help her again. But a lift home meant she could be curled up on her sofa in twenty minutes instead of standing in the cold at the mercy of public transport.

'Sure. Let me grab my coffee first.' She carefully lifted the cup, looked at the contents and poured it back into the tray. 'On second thoughts, I'll make a fresh one when I get home.'

When she didn't automatically move to follow him, Rob rested his hand at the small of her back and nudged her forward. That slight contact buzzed her into action quicker than a tip-off on a dodgy politician. Either she'd developed some sort of allergic reaction to this man, or there was serious chemistry happening between them. Hopefully, she wasn't the only one who could feel it.

'Cheers for the lift. I hope I'm not taking you too far out of your way.' Jessica showered Rob with apologetic gratitude as they sped along the motorway towards home. She'd have to add driving lessons to the list of precautions to take before her next project, along with making sure to eat regular meals and steering clear of too-close-for-comfort subject matter. At least that way she stood a chance of avoiding a repeat of today's damsel-in-distress routine.

'Not at all. Which way now?' Rob was much more matter-of-fact about the whole business, as if he rode in to work every day on his white horse, gathering up swooning women in his path.

When Jessica sneaked a peek across at her chauffeur, she conceded it was entirely feasible. Everything about him—from those strong, thick forearms locked out on the steering wheel to the muscular thighs tensing as he shifted through the gears—said he was a man who could keep a woman safe.

It was important to her that a distinction should be made between a hungry and emotional professional and those needy members of the female sex. She didn't want him to think she was one more in what was probably a long line of women desperate to snag him as a life partner. Her interest in men remained on a more casual basis. No, her wobbly-legs episode had been a severe reaction to intense circumstances today. It was in no way a manifestation of her yearning for a significant other to lean on.

Jessica helped Rob navigate the maze of avenues and side streets until they finally reached her apartment block. 'Thanks again for everything.'

'Don't mention it.'

'For the record, I promise to never pull the wailing woman routine on you again. I'll also pay to have the shirt I cried on dry-cleaned and I owe you cake.' That should cover all of her debts. Apart from the counselling he'd provided in between all of her mishaps.

'That's really not necessary.' He wasn't making it easy for her to even up the playing field. In her eyes, unless she found a way to repay him she was resigned to playing the weak-female role in their working relationship for the rest of her time here. A title she'd fought long and hard to break free from.

'I imagine you have a standing order at the dry-cleaners for clothes stained with mascara and tears anyway.' Given the nature of his work and his white knight complex, it was probably a hazard of the job.

'Yeah. They know me as Dr Heartbreak in Soapy Suds. I've got a loyalty card and everything.' The doctor's self-deprecating sense of humour was unexpected. Unfortunately, so was Jessica's snort of laughter.

She buried her face in her hands but it was too late to corral the piggy noise, which had Rob creasing up with laughter. The price of his friendship apparently came at the cost of her abject humiliation. From chasing barefoot after a bus, to her banshee wailing, and now her farmyard impression, he'd seen her at her absolute worst.

'Well, Dr Heartbreak, the least I can do is offer you a cuppa after everything you've done for me today.' Breaking her no-male-guests rule would be a small price to pay if small talk over a pot of tea helped her end the day with a modicum of dignity.

Rob had nothing but an empty house to rush home to but Jessica's invitation to come inside still waved up a red flag. He'd made that transition into friendship with her in the office today, albeit a different connection compared to the one he had with other acquaintances. He'd never felt the urge to hold Maria in his arms when she was having a bad day. There was a fragility about Jessica that called out to him and in that brief moment of comforting her Rob had relaxed his defences too.

It took a lot of energy to pretend that seeing Lauren and the others didn't get to him. He spent his days with other medical professionals who made it easy for him to keep that mask in place when they had to maintain a certain emotional distance from the patients too. Perhaps it was Jessica's empathetic way of interacting with her subjects which conned him into thinking he could drop his guard too.

He had hoped to abandon all thoughts of her on her doorstep once he'd fulfilled the promise to get her home. Now her offer to extend the evening made him think that she might need some company. Anyone would've been shaken up after everything she'd gone through today and there was a chance she didn't want to dwell on it alone. Wasn't he dreading doing the same thing himself? There couldn't be any harm in lending a sympathetic ear for a few minutes over a medicinal cup of tea. Especially if he could strike Jessica's welfare off the list of things which would keep him awake tonight.

'I would've done the same for anyone but if you've got any chocolate biscuits to go with the tea you can count me in.'

'I'm sure we can find something for that sweet tooth of yours.' Jessica went on ahead, leaving the front door open for Rob to follow.

The sound of a breaking dish and soft cursing led him towards the kitchen, where he found her picking up fragments of china from the tiled floor. The reasons he'd agreed to come into the apartment deserted him when he was confronted with the picture of her pert backside outlined in the tight grey fabric of her dress.

He said the first thing that came into his head that would excuse him for paying close attention to certain body parts he had no business staring at. 'It's highly recommended that you bend at the knees to prevent back pain.'

'You're off the clock now, Doctor, but I do appreciate your ongoing concern.' Jessica reached out and touched his arm as she straightened up again. Coupled with Rob's wayward thoughts, the unexpected contact practically singed his skin.

'No problem.' His eyes met hers and for a second he thought he saw his own desire reflected in those turquoise pools staring back at him. She blinked, breaking the spell and reminding Rob that all she'd offered him was a cuppa.

They managed to make the tea between them without any further inadvertent touching, which was a miracle, considering the cramped space they were working in. The living room they carried their tea and biscuits into wasn't any more spacious than the kitchen, made smaller by the collection of pictures and knick-knacks crammed in every available corner. Where one might have imagined modern furnishings and contemporary design, Rob saw comfy sofas and pretty floral patterns. It was homely and cosy, everything his house wasn't. He sipped his tea and perused the record of Jessica's life in candid photos lining the room.

The redhead with the boyish figure and short hair was a far cry from the curvaceous, glamorous woman standing before him now.

'Is this your mum and dad?' He lingered on the image of her sandwiched between a smiling middle-aged couple, taking pride of place on the mantelpiece. They looked so happy together it immediately made

Rob pine for the same close relationship he'd once had with his own parents. He'd severed all contact after the accident to start afresh in Belfast, with no ties to his past. Five years on and he was starting to see he'd made a mistake. He'd acted rashly, understandable when he'd suffered such a devastating loss, but it had only served to increase his punishment. That selfish decision to leave without explanation had come back to haunt him. Now he had no family at all to call his own.

'Yeah. Dad died not long after this was taken. Heart attack.' Jessica traced a finger over the figure of her father, whose Irish DNA she'd so clearly inherited, before wrapping both hands back around her cup.

'That must've been hard for you.' Rob knew that losing a parent was different to losing a wife and child but he clearly wasn't the only one having trouble moving on.

'It was. Is.' Jessica kicked off her shoes and folded herself into one of the two-seater settees, suddenly looking very small and weary.

She couldn't have been any more than eleven or twelve in the picture yet her pain was still there in her eyes. Rob saw the same haunted expression looking back at him every day in the mirror. It had taken him to battle his demons before he recognised it in her too.

He turned his back on the happy memories mocking them and took a seat opposite her. 'And your mum?'

'She's good, apart from her arthritis. Mum had me quite late in life, so we're dealing with a few health issues relating to her age now.'

'Does she live close by?' Rob hadn't even considered how his parents' health might've deteriorated since he'd seen them last. He was their only child and he'd failed them too because of his own selfish pride. As much as he was thinking about checking in with them again, he had concerns it could cause them more upset if he simply waltzed back into their lives after this length of time.

'Yeah. She's only a five-minute walk away. There are only the two of us left, so we've got each other's backs.' The strength of Jessica's bond with her mother was obvious in every word. Where death had brought her family closer, it had ripped his apart.

'You're an only child too? My parents always thought it would be unfair on me to have another child who needed their attention. I don't agree. I could have done with someone else to distract them.' Perhaps if he'd had a brother or sister to talk to, or act as mediator between him and his parents, matters might've been resolved sooner.

'I think Mum planned to have a big family but fate had other ideas.' Jessica shrugged but she couldn't fool him by feigning nonchalance when he'd already seen behind those shutters.

'It has a lot to answer for.' He gritted his teeth and silently cursed whatever powers had conspired to steal away his family's future too.

'What happened to your wife?' Jessica followed his train of thought and asked the question he'd been dreading. In the comfort of her living room, relaxing in a post-work chat, it had been easy to forget why he didn't put himself in this position of trading personal stories.

'Car accident.' That description could never adequately describe the ensuing carnage of that afternoon but he wasn't in a place where he was ready to discuss what had happened in any detail.

'Oh, my goodness. I'm so sorry.' There it was—the sympathetic head tilt and the wide eyes that said *Tell me more so I can weep for you.* The exact reason he refused to have this conversation any more. It was bad enough that people pitied him for losing his wife but he couldn't bear the sympathy and tears when he told them about Mollie too. He didn't deserve it.

He drained his cup and got to his feet before he said anything more. 'Thanks for the tea but I think it's time I was on my way.'

He could hear Jessica scrambling off her seat as he made his way to the door but he wasn't hanging around for her to dissect the story and make him the victim. Worse, she might just discover he wasn't the man she thought he was.

Damn it! Jessica had pushed him too far again. She'd only been trying to lend a listening ear, as he'd done for her. It upset her mother when she talked of her father and she wasn't exactly inundated with friends she could talk to. Some of the burden had lifted from her shoulders simply by having Rob to confide in and she'd wanted the same for him. His grief was evident in his refusal to talk about his late wife, not that Jessica would ever dream of forcing the information from him when she was still nursing her own heartache and secrets. It would be a shame for the evening to end on a bad note when she'd begun to get used to the idea of having a friend.

'Rob, wait.' She leaped up to say her goodbyes before he left.

He paused and gave her a chance to catch up. Standing toe to toe with him in the cramped hallway, with only the heavy tick of the wall clock to punctuate the silence, Jessica struggled to find the words she wanted to say. Especially when those liquid blue eyes blinking back at her were shimmering with hurt and loss.

'I didn't mean to make you uncomfortable. You've clearly been through a lot and I'm sorry I brought it up. I only wanted to be there for you, the way you were for me today.'

'It's okay.' He gave her a wobbly smile and battled to keep his alpha male stance even though his body language was crying out for a hug.

Tick-tock.

'Thanks again for everything.' She stood up on her tiptoes to give him a peck on the cheek.

'I'll see you tomor—' Rob turned to say goodbye at the same moment.

Their mouths met in an accidental kiss—a faux pas which could have been easily rectified if she'd apologised immediately and created some distance. Except his lips were as soft as they looked and she lingered there a little longer than was probably socially acceptable.

'Sorry.' She stepped back when common sense kicked in again. Kissing Rob when all he'd done was be nice to her was a stupid, impulsive move which screamed desperation.

Rob shot out his hand to catch her around the waist and pull her back. She was mid-gasp and flush against him when his mouth came crashing back down on hers.

He stole her breath away as he caught her bottom lip between his, and sent her head spinning from the lack of oxygen. She didn't know where the unexpected display of passion had come from but she wanted more. Who wouldn't want to be kissed by a hot doctor who tasted of sweet tea and salty unshed tears?

He thrust his tongue into her mouth and Jessica went limp against him, surrendering to the invasion. The sensation of butterfly wings on her skin tickled her from head to toe until every erogenous zone in her body was on high alert. She really shouldn't be enjoying this as much as she was. He was grieving. She was a mess. This felt so damn good.

Rob didn't often give in to acts of spontaneity but a chain reaction had begun within him once his lips had met hers, shutting off the rational side of his brain to let primitive instinct take over. Nothing else mattered except having another taste and her submission had given him the green light to take anything he wanted. The notion of progressing beyond a make-out session and carrying her off to bed got his blood pumping even more. She was so responsive, meeting every flick of his tongue with hers—he knew they'd be explosive together in the bedroom.

His erection was growing by the second, with Jessica pressed against him moaning her acceptance of the next step. She was trusting him with her body the way she'd trusted him with her emotions. Rob wanted her, needed her so badly it hurt—but not the complications which would come from sleeping with her. She'd shared so much with him already, she would never be simply a casual hook-up now. At some point she'd start to expect more than he could give her. The lusty haze began to clear as painful reality moved in. This was a mistake.

He must have said as much as Jessica quickly broke off the kiss.

'What?' Her desire-darkened eyes did nothing to help his current predicament.

He backed away from her. 'I don't want to make things weird between us at work. It's been a long day. We're clearly not thinking straight.'

'Right. It's been an emotional time for both of us.' She smoothed the front of her dress, creased where she'd been crushed against him, and could barely meet his eye. It was better this way. A kiss would be easier to forget than a passion-fuelled romp.

'So, we can pretend this never happened and carry on as normal tomorrow?' He always preferred to get these things straight to avoid any confusion later on. It wouldn't do either of them any good to be tiptoeing around each other for the rest of the month over a simple misunderstanding. They'd stupidly acted on their attraction instead of ignoring it but it wasn't too late to fix this.

'Sure. I mean we're not kids. One kiss is nothing to lose our heads over.'

'Right.'

They were both nodding their heads and shuffling their feet in an awkward dance around the truth. If it meant so little, they probably wouldn't feel the need to explain it away, but it suited Rob fine that they both kept up the pretence.

'I guess I'll see you tomorrow, then. Goodnight, Jessica.' He opened the front door and walked away before he did something he'd really regret.

CHAPTER FOUR

NOT EVEN THE NEWS that someone in the production crew had accidentally smashed a light fitting with a boom mike could dampen Jessica's spirits this morning. She'd spent all night replaying that Hollywood moment when Rob had pulled her back into his arms for a second kiss. It proved the attraction between them definitely wasn't one-sided even though they'd agreed to put it behind them.

That warm glow started inside her again at the mere memory. It had been a while since anyone had kissed her so passionately, made her feel so desirable, and she could easily get used to it. He'd treated her as a normal woman, not some pale, inadequate version of one. When the chemotherapy had robbed her of her beautiful hair, she'd thought no one would ever find her attractive again. At a time when friends were discovering make-up and boys, she'd been the pitiful creature tied to her sickbed, crying herself to sleep at night.

Adam had been her first serious adult relationship and since she'd been in remission when they'd met she'd been able to give everything of herself to him. Only for her useless body to let her down again and push him away when she'd needed him most. The menopause had zapped her energy, her libido and everything which had made her the woman she'd grown into.

They hadn't discussed children even after their engagement, each seemingly happy to focus on their careers. Or so she'd thought. The onset of early menopause had changed everything.

Her cycle had always been irregular but the irony of the situation was she'd thought she'd fallen pregnant when her periods stopped for good. For a short time she'd got used to the idea of being a mother and imagined having that little life growing inside her. It had been a double blow when she'd discovered the truth. After numerous negative pregnancy results and a battery of blood tests, her doctor confirmed his suspicion that she was still suffering the after-effects of her chemotherapy treatment. The high dosage of drugs she'd been exposed to for so long had finally stopped her ovaries from functioning as they should.

Neither of them had been able to handle the news that she would never be able to have a child of her own. The difference was, Adam still had the chance to walk away and start over. She didn't blame him for taking it.

The only consolation was that he hadn't been around to watch the humiliation of her going through HRT. Hormone replacement therapy might have reduced her symptoms but it didn't make a woman in her twenties feel any less of a failure. She'd had four years of dealing with this on her own and coming to terms with what it meant for her. There had been a few dalliances along the way but long-term relationships were no longer an option for her. She wouldn't let anyone get that close to her again and risk a rejection when things got serious after it had taken this long to learn to love herself again. Although she'd settle for a few more confidence-boosting smooches from Rob if he ever fancied a repeat performance of last night.

Neither of them were in the right frame of mind for anything serious when they were both carrying wounds from their past. That didn't mean they couldn't have a little fun for the duration of filming. All she had to do now was see if she could interest him in keeping things casual. More stolen kisses and passionate embraces with no ties or expectations sounded like the ideal set-up to her.

She had hoped to have caught him for another lift this morning so they could discuss what had happened but there'd been no sign of him. As she walked into the Teenage Cancer Unit to join the camera crew, she discovered why.

The unit was a separate ward for the older children, designed to have more of a relaxing vibe than the main hospital. The brightly coloured communal area, complete with comfy sofas and game consoles, resembled more of a youth club than a ward for sick children. There, in the middle of the room, Rob was already halfway through a game of pool with Cal, her lead story today. Apparently the doctor had had an earlier start than usual.

Jessica could have spent all morning watching Rob as he bent over the table, his black trousers taut around his backside, but the camera crew might've had something to say on the matter.

She walked over to view proceedings from a more respectable, if less intriguing, angle. 'Hey, you two.'

'Hi, Jessica.' Cal was first to greet her with his big beaming smile. Jessica was sure the handsome sixteen-year-old had broken the hearts of quite a few teenage girls before he'd become ill. Now he'd had the all-clear to go home again there would inevitably be a few more.

'Hey.' Rob barely lifted his head to acknowledge her before going on to pot another ball. It wasn't the scorching reunion she'd anticipated after a night reliving his hot goodbye. Even in the presence of a third party she'd expected him to be a tad friendlier towards her. Whilst she'd paid nothing more than lip service to their agreement to forget the kiss, he'd apparently followed it to the letter.

'How're you feeling today?' She focused her attention back on Cal instead of herself. His recovery was the reason she was here today and that was more important than a romance that apparently only existed in her head.

'Fine. As soon as I win a game against Dr Campbell, I'll be packing my bags for home.' There was no denying his excitement at the prospect as he high-fived his opponent. It was a far cry from the weak youngster she'd met a week ago when he'd been recovering from a virus. The chemotherapy weakened the immune system so much that even an innocuous cold was enough to floor a patient.

Jessica knew that desperation he had to get back to his own bed and belongings. The worst time for her had been when she'd had to spend Christmas on the ward, too sick to eat dinner or open presents. Cancer robbed people of more than their health; it stole childhood memories along with it. She was happy to see at least one of the children going home and getting back to his normal life.

'In that case you could be waiting awhile.' Rob showed no mercy as he cleared the table for another victory.

'You think he'd go easy and let me win one game.'

Cal shook his head and started to rack the balls up again. That stubborn determination would serve him well in the fight against his illness.

'Hey. You're the one who said you were fed up with people treating you like an invalid—' This time Rob gave Jessica a sly wink which said he was merely proving a point to Cal, not trying to hustle him.

She shuddered as her imagination went into overdrive, wishing that look was solely for her. A secret sign he was thinking about last night. It wasn't fair that this man was able to turn her inside out with one blink of an eye.

'You would have stood a better chance against me. I haven't as much as picked up a cue before.'

'It's dead easy. Here.' Cal thrust a cue into her hand and volunteered her as Rob's next challenger.

'I'm sure the doctor has better things to do than teach me how to play pool.' She tried to hand it back but Cal dodged away. Perhaps it was his way of getting out of another thrashing while still saving face. In which case she had no choice but to join in the game.

'I have a few minutes to spare before my next outpatient clinic.' Rob checked his watch but he was so hard to read; Jessica wondered if he was simply killing time or he genuinely wanted to hang out with her. Her ego wanted it to be the latter so her idea of a fling wouldn't come completely out of left field.

'So, you put your hand on the table and sort of see-saw the cue between your thumb and your forefinger.' Cal directed her first, standing with his arms folded across his chest until she did as she was told.

'Like this?'

'It's better if you make your fingers into an arch rather than have them flat on the table. Here, let me show you.' Rob came around the table to stand behind her. He leaned over and took her hands in his to demonstrate the correct posture. As his breath fanned the sensitive skin on her neck and his chest pressed against her back, Jessica was in danger of spontaneously combusting.

With his hands guiding hers she took her first shot and sank a red.

'See, it's easy. It's all about the angles.' His voice was husky in her ear, calling the hairs on the back of her neck to attention. Her imagination could've been working overtime but she thought he lingered with his arms around her for a fraction longer than he should have if she was a mistake never to be repeated.

She turned her head to thank him, only to find his mouth a few millimetres from hers. Given the hungry way he was gazing at her lips, there was every chance of another misdemeanour. A slight head tilt and they would fit together perfectly. Her breath hitched. It really was all about the angles.

'The very people I'm looking for. Cal, we need to take some more bloods before you go.' At the sound of Maria's voice in the room, Rob dropped Jessica so quickly she almost face-planted onto the table.

'Ugh. That's something I definitely won't miss.' Cal's shoulders slumped when he was faced with Maria's tools of the bloodsucking trade. Although giving blood samples became an everyday occurrence for inpatients and they were a vital part in the treatment, they certainly didn't get any easier to do. Jessica still winced when she had hers taken during her check-ups.

'Do you want to do it here, or—'

'We can do it in my room. I might have a lie-down after.'

Jessica's cheeks burned as she realised that her Rob

haze had blinded her to the fact that Cal was beginning to wilt. On closer inspection, he did seem more subdued than when she'd first arrived. It was easy to forget that even such a small thing as a game of pool could still wipe out a chemo-tired body, regardless of the strength of the spirit. Now that his cancer was in remission, hopefully he would recover quickly.

'You get your head down for forty winks and we'll get the crew to you when you're ready.' She could reorganise the running for today's shoot until he felt well enough to face the cameras with his parents. Despite whatever Rob or anyone else might think, the welfare of these kids took priority over her schedule. That was one of the perks of being top dog when they were dealing with such sensitive issues. A different producer might not have been as sympathetic to the children as one who'd gone through this herself.

Cal gave her the thumbs-up before he headed back to his room. Maria stopped halfway down the corridor and walked back towards them. For a moment, Jessica worried she was coming to give them a ticking off for tiring him out. Or to remind her that this wasn't the place to indulge her romantic fantasies.

'Rob, I wanted to make sure you're still on for tonight.'

Instead, the voluptuous Maria made her own overtures to the doc without any hesitation. The green-eyed monster tapped Jessica on the shoulder and rolled its sleeves up to prepare for a fight.

Except Rob was smiling and nodding to confirm Maria's plans.

'Of course. I wouldn't miss it for the world.'

'Good. I'll see you there at the usual time, then. Jessica, I'll give you a shout when Cal's parents come in so you can get set up.' Maria was so confident, so efficient, there was no room for argument.

'Thanks,' Jessica mumbled as Maria strode away again. Her thoughts about Rob were even more of a muddle now when clearly he and Maria had a relationship which extended outside of the hospital. There was no point in sharpening her claws over a man she had no claim on but he shouldn't have kissed her the way he had unless it meant something. She had to find out if there was something going on between Rob and the nurse before she let herself believe she had a chance with him.

Rob was glad of Maria's interruption. It dissipated the sexual tension radiating between him and Jessica. There'd been enough of that last night and he was still trying to figure out what to do about it. Every time he had her in his arms he seemed to lose his mind and that was the very reason he'd been trying to avoid her. Then she'd shown up in all her Audrey Hepburnesque glamour, ponytail swinging and eyelashes fluttering, to undo all his good work.

A gentleman would've chauffeured her to work again this morning and saved her from the horrors of public transport. Then again, a gentleman wouldn't have pounced on her the way he had last night. He'd acted on pure lust with no thought of the consequences of lunging at her like an overexcited prom date.

They'd shared a lot over the course of the evening, probably too much. For a moment he'd forgotten he would have to face her at work for the foreseeable future. She already knew too much about him to qualify as a one-night stand and starting something more than that was equally unthinkable. Even if she was agreeable.

At least he'd pulled on the brakes before doing something really stupid.

If he ever deigned to get involved again beyond a one-night fling, it would be with someone safe. Someone who wasn't always chasing the next thrill. He'd learned his lesson the hard way that family should always come before work. Perhaps he might still have his daughter with him if he and Leah had remembered that. Should he ever get a second chance at being a husband and father again, he'd strive to put that right. Only a partner with similar ideals could give him that feeling of completeness back. He was certain that someone wasn't Jessica.

'I should really get back to Outpatients.' He chose to ignore the herd of white elephants charging through the room.

'Are we really not gonna talk about what happened?'

He should've known Jessica wouldn't give him an easy out. Her style was much more confrontational.

'It was one kiss that shouldn't have happened. Let's face it—nothing was ever going to come of it. We have to work together and I don't want to complicate things. It's better if we just leave it in the past.' He glanced furtively around, as though they were discussing a matter of great national importance. In reality, he didn't want to give Maria any ammunition in her attempt to get him and Jessica together.

There was no doubt they had chemistry but Rob wouldn't be able to walk away with a clear conscience now he'd seen how delicate she was beneath the surface. His casual approach to relationships wouldn't work for her, or him, on this occasion.

'Of course. You're free to enjoy your night without worrying I'll say anything.' Jessica tilted her chin up with an air of superiority Rob didn't think was justified. They'd both acted rashly and he was simply trying to make working together less…awkward.

'I'm not sure a roomful of ten-year-old girls would be that interested in my love life but I appreciate the sentiment.'

Jessica plucked invisible dirt from her cute pink belly top and brushed her hands down her black swing skirt. 'I overheard you and Maria making arrangements for later.'

'Yeah. She railroaded me into giving a first-aid demonstration to her Girl Guide troop. You didn't think… We're nothing more than friends.' Although Rob's relationship with religion was strained these days, he was often roped in to help with church events, courtesy of his friend. He didn't mind. If he was pushed, he'd say he enjoyed the odd game of football at the youth club or chaperoning on Sunday school outings. Even though he was no longer a dad himself, supervising the kids somehow kept him connected to the role. He didn't know what that had to do with Jessica. Unless…

'Are you jealous?' Despite all his reservations about starting anything with her, he wasn't averse to the flattery of the situation.

'I didn't know… I thought that's why you didn't want me… It's none of my business anyway…' Jessica was gesticulating wildly as her cheeks glowed with a scarlet hue but he could read her as clearly as a front-page ad in the *Belfast Telegraph*.

'Maria and I have never been anything other than friends. She's more like a protective big sister than anything. Besides, I don't get involved with work colleagues. Which is exactly why that kiss between us should never have happened.' That didn't mean he hadn't wanted it but still, it was a mistake he couldn't afford to make again.

'Sure. Sure.' She was nodding now and avoiding eye contact. Telltale signs that he'd managed to screw this up even more.

'Tonight really is just a favour.' Rob didn't want them to revert to their former sparring ways on account of his actions. They could still be friends.

'You know, the director has been on my back about getting more footage of the staff outside the hospital to make them more relatable to the viewer. Do you think we could film a segment of you and Maria working with the Guides? It would really give us a contrast between your working life and what you do in your downtime.'

Jessica's proposal took him by surprise. Not least because it entailed them spending more time together outside office hours. Something which completely went against his decision to keep his distance from her.

'I wouldn't be comfortable with a film crew following me twenty-four hours a day. Besides, it would disrupt the girls too much and they're difficult to wrangle at the best of times.' This was outside the board's jurisdiction, so he had every right to say no to further intrusion. The trouble was, he'd already done Jessica a disservice by trying to pretend the kiss had never happened. Guilt often prompted him into agreeing to things which would normally be outside his comfort zone. It was the debt he felt he owed to Maria for taking him under her wing which had led him to volunteer in the first place.

'I promise we could do it with the minimum of fuss. All it would take would be a few shots at the start of the night. No muss, no fuss. Of course, I'll make sure we get consent from the children's parents before we start filming.'

'You'd have to check with Maria first.' Although Rob knew she wouldn't hesitate to agree in her endless quest to see him paired off.

'I'll do that now. Does that mean you're on board?' Jessica was the picture of innocence as she batted her eyelashes at him. And very difficult to say no to.

'I suppose I could do with another child wrangler at my side—' Rob had seen the rapport she'd built with the children here, so he trusted her to treat this as more than just another filming op.

'And I could do with brushing up on my first-aid skills.'

'In that case, I'll pick you up at seven.' Rob caved. With a roomful of giggly Girl Guides to keep him and Jessica busy, he didn't reckon they could get into too much trouble.

The 'visitor' sticker slapped on Jessica's chest wasn't merely a reminder of her status at the church hall; it was also a comment on her temporary role in Rob's life. No matter what feverish plans she might have had in mind for him, he'd made it clear he wasn't interested. If only his actions in her hallway hadn't said differently, she might have believed him.

For a split second when she'd seen him and Maria together, she feared she'd been spurned in favour of another woman. That dark cloud of self-doubt had begun to move in again, causing her to question her femininity. Despite Rob's ignorance about her fertility issues, she'd wondered if she'd still been found lacking next to the senior staff nurse. The knowledge that Rob simply didn't want her didn't make it any easier to stomach.

It was difficult not to take Rob's rejection personally but at least he'd asked her to come along with him tonight, so he wasn't averse to her company. Although this hadn't turned out to be the spontaneous, sizzling affair she'd imagined, a flicker of hope remained that spending time together might spark it to life.

She needed to know that, despite her inadequacies, she was capable of passion and evoking it in others. Her libido had taken a knock with her confidence but they both seemed to be getting back on track with Rob's help. She wasn't asking for romance and promises that couldn't be kept. All she wanted was a release for her pent-up desires and confirmation of his for her. If that didn't happen, the best she could hope for was that the friendly neighbourhood oncologist currently giving up his free time to babysit a group of Girl Guides might actually convince her there were some good guys out there.

'He's like a rock star when he comes here.' Maria stood at the back of the small room with Jessica, keeping an eye on proceedings. She was every bit as authoritative out of the hospital setting, even if she was in her casual wear rather than her uniform.

'Does he come here often?' It wasn't supposed to come out as a cheesy pick-up line from the seventies but Jessica was intrigued by the easy relationship he apparently had with everyone here.

She hadn't met many single professional men with the ability to talk to children on their level without being patronising and Rob's laughter said this was something he did for fun, not as a chore.

Until coming to the hospital, she'd never spent a lot of time with children. It was difficult being around other people's babies knowing she could never have one of her own. The nature of Rob's work meant he had a lot of experience dealing with them and it showed as he got them warmed up with a few parlour games. It was no wonder that a man who probably had family on his mind for the future wouldn't be interested in a fling.

Regardless of the inner strength Jessica had built up since her wedding dreams had ended, the longing for that perfect family life would probably never leave her either.

'Yes, he helps us out with the kids' clubs quite often, though he's never brought a friend with him before.' Maria's gaze flickered between Rob and Jessica. She'd become animated the minute they'd walked into the hall together. Unfortunately, there was absolutely no reason for anyone to get excited.

'As I said earlier, the director thought it would be good to get an idea of what our revered physician does outside of the department to show his fun side. Thanks for helping me get all the consent forms sorted out so quickly, by the way.' The director had actually said they needed to 'humanise' the man who dealt with life and death every day. Jessica had argued in the firm belief they'd captured his compassion perfectly but she'd consented that it would be nice to see more of him as a person in his own right.

She'd been reluctant to pitch the idea to Rob, given his initial reaction to filming the documentary, but Maria and the Guides had given her the perfect opportunity. It would be fair to say curiosity had also got the best of her about what he and Maria did together here.

'No problem. I'm stunned Rob agreed to this in the first place. He's a very private man.'

Jessica understood that fierce need to maintain control over personal information. Thankfully, the few relationships she'd had to date had been so one-dimensional she'd never had to reveal her personal shame.

Rob was different. He'd already found a way to get her to open up and that should've been the signal to cut her losses and walk away. For some reason, Rob made her want to stick around and figure out what made him tick too.

'I think he understands how important this is to the programme. I'm very grateful to you both for agreeing to do this.' Jessica didn't want to read too much into Rob's decision to take part when her hopes had already been dashed once on that front. She had to go with the positives that he was happy to work with her and that solved her professional dilemma if not her personal one.

As promised, after getting a few shots of Rob playing with the children, Jessica was able to send the crew on their way again. The footage, along with the long-awaited interview, should be enough personal insight into the man of the moment to keep the director happy. Even if she personally hankered for more.

Once all the recording equipment had been packed away and Jessica and Maria were the only spectators left, they fell into an uneasy silence while the rest of the room echoed with excited chatter around them. The girls were swarming around Rob as he produced a selection of bandages and splints from his medical bag.

He clapped his hands together to cut across the din. Playtime was over. 'Okay, can everyone please find a partner?'

The pack immediately followed his command and separated into pairs, all patiently waiting for further instruction.

'He is completely oblivious to the effect he has on young girls. I'm sure there's more than one who's developed a crush on him.' Maria watched him like a proud mother, putting all of those misconceptions about their relationship to rest.

Jessica forced a laugh, since she counted herself as one of those afflicted and was probably doing as bad a job at hiding it.

They listened to Rob give a short introduction about first aid and why it was necessary to think of personal safety as well as that of the casualty. He was adept at both fielding questions and making sure the girls understood the importance of the steps before attempting any treatment. 'I'm going to show you a few skills which might be helpful in the event of an accident. Of course, if there's a serious injury involved you should dial 999. Now, I'm going to need a volunteer to help me with the demonstration.'

A dozen eager hands shot into the air.

'Jessica?' He waved her to the front of the hall and Maria gave her a little shove forward into the spotlight.

She could feel the jealous eyes of every girl upon her as she made her way to Rob's side. 'I don't think I'm the right person for this. I thought I'd be handing out bandages and pouring orange squash.'

'You're perfect,' he whispered back, stealing her objection with a well-timed compliment. It was far from the truth; nevertheless, it had the desired effect on her. The idea of him accepting her, regardless of her flaws, set her heart aflutter and turned her brain to mush. Apparently those two little words were capable of reducing her from a strong, independent woman to just another love-struck girl.

'Now, lie on the floor for me.'

Her dreamy moment took a nightmarish turn.

'Pardon me?'

'I want to demonstrate the recovery position and I

can only do that if you kindly lie down. Please.' It was the plea at the end with a trace of panic which finally broke her down. This wasn't some sort of sick revenge for disrupting her workplace; he was asking her for help and she owed him big-style. She wouldn't let him down for the sake of her own pride.

'Fine.' Thank goodness she'd swapped her flouncy skirt for jeans or this could've been even more awkward. She thought she heard Rob's sigh of relief when she complied and fell at his feet for the second time that week.

Her pulse was racing as he knelt at her side.

'Try to relax,' he said as he unfurled her balled-up hands and moved her arms to her sides.

'That's easier said than done when I'm lying here at your mercy.' And wishing it was in altogether very different circumstances. Everything she'd seen of Rob at work said he was loving and giving and that was bound to extend to other areas of his life.

Jessica's mind wandered towards the bedroom and what a considerate lover he would make.

'I'll be gentle.'

The whispered words in her ear sent an all-points bulletin to body parts south of the border as arousal flooded through her. This was torture. Sweet, sweet torture.

'I'm feeling a bit hot.' The urge to flirt with him became too great to ignore. She wanted him to acknowledge that he wasn't as immune to her as he appeared.

'You do look flushed. Do you want me to loosen your top button?'

She bit her lip as she nodded. At this moment in time all she wanted was for him to touch her.

It might have been wishful thinking on her part that

his bright blue eyes had darkened to glittering sapphires as his fingers brushed the delicate skin at her throat but she really wanted him to rethink the boundaries on their relationship. She swallowed hard as he opened her blouse.

'Better?'

'Better,' she agreed even though she was burning from the inside out.

'I need you to close your eyes. You're supposed to be unconscious.'

Jessica was reluctant to block out the image of him smiling down at her as if they were the only people in the room, but she did as he asked of her.

All other senses heightened to compensate for the loss of her sight, the smell of his rich, woody aftershave enveloping her as he leaned over her. Rob explained to their audience that the recovery position was used for those who were unconscious but breathing, and only used if the person didn't have a neck or spiral injury.

'The first thing we want to do is check that the patient is responsive, by gently shaking and calling out to them. Jessica, are you awake?' Rob placed his hands on her shoulders and shook her.

How could she play the unresponsive patient when every part of her was tingling with sexual awareness? Had she known she'd spend her Friday night lying on a cold, dusty floor pretending she was unfazed by his every touch she might've found alternative entertainment for the evening. Although getting this close to him would be an incentive to do anything.

'If there is no response, call for help and move on to the next stage of checking the airways are open and clear. With an unconscious patient you can do this by tilting their head and lifting their chin.' Rob's hands were firm as he moved her into position. In her daydream she imagined this as her Sleeping Beauty moment with Rob playing the handsome Prince, come to kiss her into consciousness.

'Check the breathing now. Look for the chest rising and falling, feel the breath on your cheek or listen for the sounds.' Rob's breath was warm on her face, his mouth as close to hers as it could be without touching. She wondered if he could tell her breathing was *actually* becoming shallow. Perhaps if she acted her part well enough he'd give her mouth to mouth and put her out of her misery.

'If the person is breathing, then it is safe to move them into the recovery position until help arrives. Put the arm closest to you at a right angle to their body, with the palm facing upwards. Move the palm of their other hand against their chest. Lift the knee furthest from you so their leg is bent and their foot is flat on the floor. You can roll the person onto their side by pulling the bent knee towards you.' Rob manipulated Jessica's limbs so she moved at his will. Clearly she was long overdue some physical intimacy with the opposite sex for her to find this as erotic as she did. It wasn't often that she relinquished control but there was something about this man that made her trust him. That would make an interesting development in her love life, even if it was playing with fire.

'Rest the head on the free hand, with the mouth pointed towards the floor in case the patient should vomit. Make sure you push the chin away from the chest and keep the knee bent at a right angle to their body. Check breathing again while you wait for an ambulance.'

There was a whoosh of cold air around Jessica's

body and a sense of loss as Rob apparently got back to his feet.

'I want to see you take turns in your teams, repeating the process and talking me through the steps.'

Jessica opened one eye and squinted up at him. 'Can I get up now?'

'Sure. A round of applause, please, for my glamorous assistant.' Rob reached out to help her up. Jessica wobbled as she got back to her feet and steadied herself with a hand on his chest. In that instant back in his arms, they recreated that heat they'd had in her hallway. She recognised that lust in Rob's eyes as he stared down at her; it was the same thing coursing through her veins.

The clapping from the crowd grew so loud she knew there was no choice for them but to break apart. Jessica took a bow but secretly hoped this wasn't the final curtain. As far as this thing with Rob was concerned, she was waiting for an encore performance.

'Jessica, could you give me a hand going over the steps with the girls?' Rob called her back into action before she let her rampant imagination carry her too far away.

For the next twenty minutes she mingled with the pairs, helping them to remember the positions before Rob would give them one last test. In amongst the serious attempts to impress the instructor, there were also moments of fun as the group began to treat Jessica as one of their own. She fell into the role of agony aunt as they came to her seeking advice on boys and fashion, despite her warning she wasn't an expert on either subject. The innocence and honesty of the group was refreshing for someone who spent her time with cynical television types.

She'd forgotten what it was like to be part of something

fun without having to worry about the other parties' motives. Rob's participation in the activities here was beginning to make sense. Outside the pressure of work, this was the perfect place to unwind and still make a difference to the community. In some ways the split from Adam had turned her into the same self-serving monster she'd run from. Whilst she'd been cautious to protect herself from further hurt, she'd also been selfish, never taking into consideration how she could help others. Rob had suffered a tragedy which made her situation pale in comparison but he wasn't drowning in a sea of self-pity; he was still making a difference in other people's lives. Hers included.

CHAPTER FIVE

In amongst the throng of excited would-be doctors, Jessica noticed one young girl doubled over at the side of the room.

'Miss, I don't think Ciara's feeling very well.' The girl's partner confirmed Jessica's suspicions as she made her way over to the pair.

'Ciara? Do you need to sit down?' Jessica pulled a chair over and guided her into it. As soon as she saw the girl's grey pallor and heard her gasping for air, she knew it was time to call for help. 'Rob, I need you over here. Now!'

He was there in seconds, kneeling in front of the child and taking both of her hands in his. 'I need you to take long, deep breaths, Ciara. In and out.'

After a few controlled breaths the initial panic for all concerned began to subside. Maria distracted the rest of the girls with a promise of orange juice and biscuits once Rob assured her that he and Jessica could deal with the patient.

'Good girl, Ciara. Now, do you have your inhaler?' Rob's knowledge of the girl's condition said a lot about his relationship with those who attended the church. He was clearly more adept at making friends than Jessica had given him credit for.

Ciara nodded and produced the blue inhaler from her pocket. Rob shook it and uncapped it so she could take a couple of puffs to relieve her symptoms. They waited and listened as her breathing slowly regulated.

'We should really get you home, sweetheart.' Jessica rubbed her back and looked to Rob for further instruction. It was bound to be a frightening experience for Ciara every time her asthma flared up. Illness at that age was never easy and Jessica knew when she was sick the only place she wanted to be was tucked up in her own bed.

'I'll phone your mum and let her know what's happened. Jessica and I can give you a lift home if she agrees to it. Okay?' As soon as he got the go-ahead, Rob went off to make the call and Jessica did her bit to pacify Ciara until his return. She had to admit there were certain areas where she was willing to submit to his authority and she didn't let that happen with just anyone.

He was a take-charge kind of guy but he did it without arrogance or superiority. Nothing seemed to rattle him and she couldn't help wishing she'd had someone like him beside her when her world had been ripped out from beneath her. Things might have been different if she'd had a partner willing to be with her at any cost.

Rob called an end to the class. Now he had permission from Ciara's parents to take her home, he gave her another check-over and made sure she wrapped up before they headed out into the night. She was supposed to have been picked up by a friend of her mother's when the class was over but he felt more comfortable taking her himself in case of another attack.

It wasn't the first time he'd dealt with Ciara's asthma but the difference here was Jessica's support, for him and his patient. Instead of going into meltdown and causing Ciara to panic in return, she'd stayed calm and helped control the situation. There were no cameras rolling, no bosses to impress and no monetary gain to justify her actions. Her sole concern had been for Ciara's welfare and again that truly screwed with his idea that all media types were incapable of human emotion.

Bit by bit she was decimating his defences. Even now, with all three of them in his car, she was constantly reaching out to Ciara in the back seat to make sure she was warm enough and making small talk to keep her mind off her asthma. That sort of bedside manner would've made her a good doctor if she'd ever thought of following that path. Perhaps it was her choice of profession which had skewed his view of her from the start.

There was no escaping the incredible chemistry they had together. He was almost embarrassed about the display they'd put on during the demonstration, when he'd found every excuse he could for touching her. Perhaps it was because he'd tagged her as forbidden fruit, which made her all the more appealing. Denying himself something, someone who could give him so much pleasure only increased his appetite for it. He was craving Jessica the way a dieter craved carbs and chocolate. Given her sultry looks and breathy responses to his every touch when she was supposed to be unconscious, he didn't think she was against the idea either.

It was approaching the time when he might have to admit there was something going on and stop putting up imaginary barriers between them. Even the strictest dietary regimes left room for the odd lapse.

He parked as close as he could to Ciara's house so the cold night didn't trigger another attack. Jessica was first out of the car to help their patient and they both escorted her to the front door. Rob was acquainted with Ciara's mother but he was sure she appreciated having a female presence arrive with her daughter too. They refused the invitation for a cup of tea and he left his charge with instructions to watch her closely and phone the doctor in the morning.

'I'm sorry I ruined everything.' Ciara hung her head as they said their goodbyes but Rob couldn't let her go to bed burdened with so much unnecessary guilt.

'Not at all. We can pick it up again next week when you've all had time to practice.' That seemed to perk her up again, so he was free to leave with a clear conscience too.

'Will Jessica be there too?' Ciara's question left Rob and his new assistant staring at each other for the answer.

'If she wants to…' Rob didn't want to put her on the spot but he had no clue where things would stand in a week's time. She didn't need any more footage, so the answer would depend entirely on whether or not she wanted to spend her free time with him and a bunch of Girl Guides.

'I'd love to.'

Rob matched Jessica's grin as she committed to another evening with him. He was obviously a masochist when he was looking forward to another round of *Let's pretend we don't want to rip each other's clothes off.*

As they made their way back to the car, Jessica seemed to lose some of the spring in her step.

'Is there something wrong?'

She exhaled a slow breath, sending wisps of white whirling into the atmosphere. 'I just know how horrible it is to have to deal with that at her age.'

'You had asthma too?' A lot of things began to fall

into place for Rob. If Jessica had spent her childhood in and out of hospital, it would explain her empathy with the children. There was a possibility he'd mistaken her passion for the subject matter as naked ambition. Her admission changed his perception of her even more. Although she would probably see it as a weakness. It made him all the more privileged that she chose to share the information with him.

'Not asthma, but yeah, I was a sick kid.' It was a flat statement of fact with no plea for sympathy attached. Yet, as a doctor, Rob's interest was automatically piqued. Jessica was a fighter and he couldn't imagine her succumbing to anything, including illness.

'With any luck, Ciara's condition will improve as she gets older. I assume that's what has happened in your case?' He hadn't seen any residual physical evidence of whatever had ailed her. Except for the freckles left where the sun had kissed her nose, there were no scars or blemishes on her skin that he could see. And he'd been studying her form very closely these past few days. He knew her aquamarine eyes flashed with amber when she was annoyed and her cheeks flushed red when he was near.

'Yes, but recovery was long and not without challenges. I hope she does get better but sickness taints everything when you look back on those lost years. Hospital beds and blood tests aren't the stuff of nostalgic childhood memories. See, it's left me bitter and twisted.' Her humourless laugh was more disturbing than the sight of her unshed tears glistening in the darkness of the car. Whatever battle she'd fought had clearly left more than physical scars. Despite all his medical training, Rob had never found the magic cure for emotional trauma. If he had, he might have found it easier to open up the way Jessica could with him.

'And everything's okay now?' He didn't want to dig any deeper than she was comfortable with about her condition but if there was anything he could do for her in a professional capacity he wouldn't hesitate to do so.

'Yeah. I got the all-clear a long time ago.' There was a long pause, as if she was debating whether or not to go into further detail. Rob held off on starting the car ignition in case it broke the spell. He wanted to know what had happened in her past to haunt her still. He wanted to help her through it.

'Childhood leukaemia. Acute lymphoblastic leukaemia, to be precise.'

Rob's breath caught in his throat. He'd seen many patients suffering that particular condition. ALL was such a devastating illness, with an average length of treatment of around two years. A long time snatched from a childhood, to be spent in and out of hospitals. 'You've been through the wars, all right.'

'I'm a survivor, if nothing else. My heart goes out to Ciara. The fight is never easy.' With everything else Jessica had been through, she was entitled to feel sorry for herself once in a while but she'd reserved her pity for another little girl. She was a remarkable woman who'd overcome so much and if she ever decided to give motivational talks Rob would be the first to sign up. Perhaps there was something to be said for this unburdening of personal problems. After all, he'd slept a little better himself after finally telling someone about Leah. It was a type of therapy without paying a stranger to listen, or being tagged as a patient. Still, her empathy for others meant she was taking on other worries she could do nothing about.

'I know but you're here and you're healthy now. There's no reason why Ciara can't have that in the future too.'

'You're right. I'm just being silly.' Jessica reached for her seat belt and indicated she was ready to go.

'Not at all. You're caring and sympathetic. A beautiful person, inside and out.' In his mind, Rob was reaching out to her, cradling her face in his hands and kissing her. It was his heart telling him he shouldn't. The only thing he knew for certain was that he didn't want her to go home just yet. He couldn't dump her out of the car after she'd laid herself bare to him.

He hadn't been in this position before. Sure, he'd done his fair share of counselling families in the course of his job, but this was different. Jessica needed physical and emotional support and he wasn't sure he was capable of giving one without the other. If he kissed her, it would take them to a level beyond friendship and he didn't want that when she was so emotionally vulnerable.

He should really confess his sins and put her off from wanting anything from him at all, but he didn't want to do it here in the dark where they could barely see each other's faces.

'Thanks.'

Rob fumbled with his keys to get the engine started and break the tense atmosphere he'd created. 'I don't live far from here if you want to go grab a bite to eat? Your day has been every bit as busy as mine and we don't want you passing out again, do we?'

'I suppose...' Jessica's judgement where men were concerned was apparently still completely out of whack to have mistaken a compliment as a come-on. For a split second she'd imagined he was going to kiss her, only to find the hungry look in his eyes was for a snack, not her. She'd told him the very thing which had defined everything about her and she took his non-reaction as another snub.

If it wasn't for her growling stomach and an evening dwelling on her misfortunes alone to look forward to, she might well have declined the invitation.

She knew she'd made the right call when they drew up into the driveway. The large chalet-style bungalow was more of a family residence than the trendy bachelor pad she'd pictured him in. It was a new build and, with the acres of empty fields surrounding it, probably more expensive than a luxury apartment in the city.

It was immaculate inside; the order and precision he displayed at work clearly extended here too.

'Make yourself…er…comfortable and I'll see what we have in the way of food.' Rob led her through to the living room.

'No problem. Give me a shout if you need a hand with anything.' She took a seat on the shiny black leather settee. Everything in the room looked as if it had just been unwrapped. He'd been here five years and the place still didn't feel lived-in. Despite Rob's devotion to his wife's memory, there were no pictures of her around, no personal artefacts visible anywhere. As if he was in denial about what had happened. It wasn't healthy.

Rob returned carrying a few paltry grocery items which did not have the makings of a gourmet meal. 'We have tinned soup, eggs, some sort of vegetables, and I'm sure I saw a packet of sausages that are only days out of the best-before date in there somewhere too.

Sorry, I didn't think this through. I could whip up an omelette if you like?'

'There's no need. I love tomato soup and it means we can be eating in less than five minutes.' Soup had been one of the few things she'd been able to stomach during her illness and she related it to a comfort of sorts. She was ready for it after the day she'd had.

'As you wish.' Rob gave a sweeping bow and backed out of the room but Jessica was keen to spend more time in his company. Especially with this playful side of him.

'Wait, I'll come and help.'

The kitchen resembled something from a show home with its marble worktops, oak units and state-of-the-art gadgets. Her whole apartment would probably fit into one corner of it too. 'Are you telling me you have *this* to cook in and your diet is that of a penniless student?'

'Give me a break. I haven't had a chance to shop yet this week.' Rob poured the thick red gloop into two bowls and set the timer on the microwave.

Jessica wasn't buying it. The kitchen was so pristine, either he never used it or he had an army of woodland creatures under his command keeping it spotless. The size of this house would emphasise anyone's loneliness and she didn't understand why he would move here in the first place after losing his wife. She found it hard enough at times to fill the silence in her poky dwelling space, never mind this sprawling country estate—population one. At least she had her mother to visit when the loneliness became too much. From her restricted view of Rob's situation, it felt as though he was punishing himself by living in this vast empty space, as far from human company as he could get. Somehow she'd achieved VIP status which allowed her access inside his hallowed sanctuary.

'I'm sure you have a lovely view from here.' Although,

without the light pollution of traffic and civilisation, all she could see at the moment was eternal darkness.

'Aye. It's the perfect spot if you're fond of fields and sheep.'

Or brooding.

As beautiful as Rob's house was, this kind of isolation was never going to help his situation and Jessica had learned long ago it wasn't healthy to hold back on what she was thinking. Dinner could wait but if she didn't get this out now she'd burst. 'Do you really think Leah would want you to hide away out here for the rest of your life?'

Rob braced himself against the worktop, his back still towards Jessica and his hackles well and truly raised. 'You don't understand.'

'You're right. I don't. So explain to me why you're so damned hard on yourself.' After everything she'd shared with him, he should be able to trust her with his story. Unfortunately, trying to get information out of him was like banging her head off a solid, muscly brick wall.

The beep from the microwave barely registered for Rob as he was forced to turn around and confront the demons he'd grown tired of hiding from. 'I couldn't save her. I failed as a doctor, a husband... I wasn't there for her when she needed me the most.'

He'd been so caught up in his work, in saving other people's lives, he hadn't been there to protect the ones who mattered most to him. If only he'd shared the excitement of his daughter and joined the shopping expedition for her first day at school instead of dwelling on the argument he'd had with Leah at home, he might've prevented the tragedy.

Rob caught himself before he blurted out about Mollie, and how he'd failed as a father too. One shameful secret at a time. He didn't want Jessica to judge him or pity him any more than she did already. It wouldn't bring his family back. More than that, the memories he had of Mollie were his alone now and he wouldn't share her with just anyone.

'It wasn't your fault. It was an accident, something you could never have foreseen.' Jessica's naivety about the situation made her kitchen psychology all the more infuriating.

'We'd had a stupid row the night before and I was still stewing over it. Otherwise, I would've been with her when the so-called joyrider ran into her. I might've prevented it.'

They'd only been together a few months when she'd fallen unexpectedly pregnant and, if Rob was honest, Mollie was probably the reason they'd married so quickly. It had been Leah's decision to put her career on hold at the time but Rob would've supported her, whatever choice she'd made. That had made her deception all the harder to swallow. There'd been no need to lie to him about what she was doing or where she was going when he would've done whatever it took to make her happy.

They'd loved each other but he'd got the impression she'd started to resent him and Mollie for stifling her dreams. She clearly hadn't been content as a stay-at-home mum and he hadn't seen it until it was too late. The discrepancy between what Rob had thought was happening whilst he was at work and the reality of how Leah spent her time only came to light when their daughter had become cranky and out of sorts. In the end the truth had come from the mouth of his baby and turned his world upside down. The lack of communication between him and Leah, his ultimate failure as a husband to recognise that his wife was troubled, had cost him everything.

'The accident might have happened regardless if you were there or not.'

'Maybe, maybe not. I don't know what Leah's state of mind was when she took off in the car and they never caught the other driver. I'll never know how the accident happened and that's the killer. There's that small chance I could've prevented the accident, or saved her if I'd been at the scene.' And saved Mollie too.

'It's a terrible thing to have to come to terms with, but you can't blame yourself when you weren't driving either car.' Jessica's simplistic view didn't leave any room for survivor's guilt, or crippling thoughts that he could've somehow changed fate.

To this day the sight of policemen in the department still brought that lurching fear in his stomach that they were coming to deliver life-shattering news.

'Unfortunately, bad things happen to good people. Don't you think I've spent a lifetime trying to find someone to blame for my problems? Did I get sick because of something I or my parents did? No, it's just one of those awful things sent to test us and make us stronger human beings. You can't spend for ever letting the accident consume you. It's not your fault.' Jessica said those words his mother had played on repeat until he could hear them no more. It didn't mean anything when newspaper headlines were there to remind him that he was the doctor who couldn't save his own family.

Jessica cupped his face in her hands, insisting he look at her. 'It's not your fault and you deserve more than this half-life you're living. This tragedy happened *to* you, not *because* of you. Trust me, I know the difference.' Jessica was as passionate as ever, defending him from his inner turmoil. He wanted to believe she was someone he had an affinity with. For a little while he wanted to escape from the inside of his head and let himself feel something other than the guilt he carried with him on a daily basis.

'It's not your fault.' She repeated the mantra and kissed him on both cheeks. Something he'd been too afraid to do to comfort her in case she read something into it. As usual, she acted without any of the introspection he got bogged down into before every single move he made.

'It's not your fault.' She kissed him on the mouth. Perhaps she thought if she said it enough he'd start to believe it. How different things would be if he could share in her delusion and imagine he was nothing more than a lonely man who needed comfort. That he had permission to feel something more than the immense sadness which engulfed his heart.

He closed his eyes and tried to block out the past to focus on the present. On the soft pressure bearing down on his lips, her exotic scent tickling his nose and that taste of excitement on his tongue.

When he thought she was moving away, he went with her, keeping their mouths fused together to prolong the moment for a while longer. She relaxed into him and Rob revelled in the warmth and comfort of her embrace. He rounded his hand over her backside and brought her flush against him to meet him at every contact point guaranteed to fry his brain for good.

'Jessica…if we don't stop this now…' His voice was ragged with desire but he didn't want to go any further and live to regret it.

'What? We've both been denying ourselves this for too long.'

Jessica went to work on the buttons of his shirt, exposing his bare skin to the cold air and her warm mouth. His nipples hardened, along with other stimulated parts of his body, as she trailed kisses over his torso. With every touch, he was hurtling away from his pain. Jessica was a better cure than a kilo of chocolate and overtime any day.

He fought to think straight as she licked her tongue around his nipple. 'I don't want to get into anything serious.'

'Me neither.' She paid more attention to what she was doing rather than what he was saying.

'I mean it. I don't go in for anything more than one night with anyone.' He wanted to establish boundaries before they were past the point of no return.

She stopped what she was doing to look him square in the eye. 'I get it. Neither of us wants to get involved. That suits me fine. Right now I'd say one night of unbridled passion will get this thing out of our systems. In a few weeks' time I'll move on with nothing more than fond memories.' Trust her to verbalise her feelings so succinctly when he was struggling to find the words. He no longer had to worry about her agenda and there were no more barriers to stop him giving in to impulse just this once.

He drew her back up along his body so he could lose himself in the taste of her again and forget all the reasons they were so wrong for each other. Here and now, they were simply two lost souls clinging together, finding comfort in each other.

With his lips and tongue meshed with Jessica's, Rob finally released the passion he'd been holding back for so long. He slid his hand under her silky white shirt and cupped her breast, brushing a thumb over her nipple to bring it to attention. That small indication of her arousal launched his own into hyperdrive. He trailed kisses along her neck and unbuttoned her shirt with his free hand, exposing more of her body for him to tend.

Jessica's moans caused another rush of blood through his veins and called to his inner caveman. He yanked her bra aside and latched his mouth around the pink tip straining to greet him. She was soft and hard, spicy and sweet, so wrong and yet so right.

Fuelled by lust and adrenaline, Rob tugged Jessica's jeans and panties down out of his way. Clearly in as much of a hurry as he was, she kicked them off and returned the favour by unzipping his fly to let him spring free. He was on board a runaway train now. Even though he wanted to enjoy the sights, he was eager to get to the final destination. As he contemplated how to delay the journey, Jessica hopped on board and took control. With her arms around his neck, her legs hooked to his hips, she anchored herself to his erection.

Rob shuddered, fighting the instant gratification as they forged their bodies together. Jessica groaned into his ear and almost finished it then and there. He stilled inside her, adjusting to the tight heat taking hold of him, before he moved again. He backed her against the kitchen worktop, resting her butt on the edge so he had her where he wanted her.

With Jessica clinging to him like a second skin, he drove into her and found his sanctuary. Every thrust drew a gasp, pulling him closer to the edge of sanity. He'd denied himself so long, he gorged on this feeling of fulfilment without respite.

She raked her nails over his scalp, riding his demons

out with him. She seemed to gauge what it was he needed, what this meant, and kept pace until he was hurtling to the finish line. Rob's breath came in pants as the pressure built up inside him to bring this to an end. She clenched her inner muscles around him, squeezing him into immediate surrender. He poured inside her, releasing all of his frustration in a primal scream. Although he might repent his actions at a later date, for now Rob didn't have a care in the world.

CHAPTER SIX

JESSICA MADE IT back to solid ground on shaky legs and adjusted her shirt to at least cover her top half. Rob had literally taken her breath away. Although she'd always had an inkling of that fire behind the ice, she'd never expected him to be *so* impulsive, *so* hot-blooded. Everything about this was reckless and wild and everything she'd wanted to get out of her system. The trouble was, she couldn't wait to stoke the flames of passion again. Now she knew how great they could be together, once would never be enough for her. The spontaneity of what had just happened showed that he genuinely desired her above all else at this moment in time, but Jessica demanded proof that this was more than a temporary lapse of judgement on his part.

The doubt was already clouding his eyes as he rebuttoned his pants. She slapped his hand away.

'What the—'

'I'm not done with you yet.' She hooked a finger into his waistband and pulled him close for a lazy kiss.

'No?'

'We agreed on one night. One *full* night.'

She led him towards the door, in search of that elusive bedroom. Rob stopped in the doorway, a dead weight she couldn't hope to move without his cooperation. She knew he was debating whether or not to follow.

'If this is a one-time deal, we really ought to make the most of it. Don't you think?' She spoke softly so as not to spook him. One wrong move and this would be over before she even got him naked.

Rob unhooked her finger and took her hand in his. 'Then what are we waiting for?'

Brass bands heralded her triumph, white doves soared into the sky, and the sun broke through the gloom with the news. Jessica had definitely got her groove back on and she couldn't wait to dance the night away with her sexy new lover.

Now the initial frenzy had passed they faced each other across the vast expanse of Rob's king-sized bed in awkward silence. She was worried they'd lose momentum if they had too much time to think about what they were doing. Her hands trembled as she removed what little there was left of her clothes. Standing here naked before him was different from getting frisky still half dressed. She didn't have her pretty clothes to express her femininity for her. She was leaving herself open to scrutiny and Rob wasn't just a random hook-up she wouldn't see again. It mattered what he thought of her. She wanted him to want her.

When it came to getting value for money, she knew she was getting a good deal. Rob worked out, a lot. From his rounded biceps to his sinewy thighs, and everything in between, he was built for pleasure. She looked forward to uncovering every toned inch.

'Heels on or off?' She strode over to him with her hands on her hips, exuding a confidence she worked damn hard to convey. The business she was in had taught her to hide any weakness beneath a layer of bravado. Her body had let her down in the past and there was no better way to hide her insecurities than to strut around in nothing but a pair of shoes.

'Definitely on.' He made a guttural sound as he all but rugby tackled her onto the bed. Jessica shrieked, secretly delighted he found her visual stimulation irresistible. With Rob covering her body entirely with his, she was able to relax a little, but there was definitely an air of born-again virgin as she lay beneath him. It had been a while since she'd slept with anyone, never mind someone she'd swapped personal sob stories with. It brought the emotional element to intimacy she usually did her best to avoid. She arched up off the bed, keen to quieten that wounded part of her, and embraced this for what it was. A night to remember.

Each movement she made brought their bodies together. Not close enough. This time she wanted the full skin-on-skin experience. In seconds, she'd stripped him bare to see and feel the full evidence of his arousal pressed against her. There was no greater aphrodisiac for her than a hunky man who made her feel desirable. More than that, lying here beneath Rob, she could stop pretending to be anything more than she was. He knew almost all of her secrets—the ones that mattered for now.

He kissed her—a long, languid seduction of her mouth, promising a more thorough exploration of her body this time around. Something which made her shiver with anticipation and trepidation. Would he still find her this sexy if he knew her illness had taken away a vital part of her femininity?

'What about protection?' The irony of Rob's raspy request brought Jessica's tears closer to the surface.

She had to swallow them down before she could answer him. This was a chance to tell him the truth but she didn't want to start another discussion about her tragic history and break the mood. It was only supposed to be a casual hook-up designed to break the sexual tension between them once and for all. Not a proposal of marriage and an expectation she could give him babies.

'I've got it covered,' she said with a smile to hide her heartache. If it wasn't for her infertility, she might have fostered the notion she could have more than a one-night stand with someone like Rob.

He lifted his head to grin back at her before starting to kiss his way down her body again. Goosebumps popped along her skin with every feather-light touch of his lips. She didn't want to hold on to any of her baggage when he was intent on making her fantasies come true. He reached up to cup her breast in his large hand, rolling her nipple into a tight peak between his thumb and finger. Jessica had to bite her lip to stop from crying out as he dipped his head and drew the sensitive tip into his warm mouth. He trailed his tongue over her, flicking and teasing until she was bucking off the mattress like a wild thing.

For tonight, at least, her body was his to command. His mouth never left her as he made his way further down the bed, scorching a trail of wet kisses along her torso. As he manoeuvred himself between her legs and dared even lower, Jessica could no longer think of anything except her own desires.

He licked the seam of her womanhood and parted her with his tongue, her liquid arousal rushing to meet him. With every lick and swirl he demanded her climax until she complied, her cries echoing through the quiet house as that all-encompassing bliss claimed her. Only when he'd drawn the final aftershocks of her release did he replace his tongue with his equally breathtaking erection.

Rob braced himself on the bed with one arm either side of her and moved slowly inside her. He was already trembling with restraint, since the intensity of her orgasm had almost claimed him too. Now every one of his senses was heightened, every nerve ending zinging with energy as they forged together. He was lost to her heat, her sexiness and this amazing feeling of being alive. Despite their mutual agreement that this was nothing more than sex, somewhere in the back of his mind he knew this was wrong. Thankfully, carnal instinct kept it at bay.

She was hugging his waist with her thighs as she rode with him, punctuating every stroke with an erotic moan. Driving him to the point of madness. His thoughts, his whole being belonged entirely to her in that moment.

She clenched her inner muscles around him, hastening him towards that glorious peak of complete satisfaction. A roar was ripped from his soul with his final release, so powerful and strong it shook him to the very core. This was more than sex; he'd held nothing back as he'd made love to Jessica and he had no clue what that meant for the future. All he did know was that this euphoria wouldn't last. Not when they had to face real life tomorrow as a busy doctor and TV producer, only thrown together under temporary circumstances.

He lay down beside her and placed a kiss on her lips, thankful that she'd helped him to spend time in the here and now. For a while, at least.

'Are you okay? You're very quiet.' She was frowning at him and he knew he'd spent too long in his own head. It wasn't very gentlemanly of him to be thinking of anything other than the amazing time they'd just shared. The urge to flog himself with birch branches and repent his sins could wait until her side of the bed was cold again.

'You've worn me out, that's all.' He reached across and stroked his thumb against her cheek, keen to maintain some physical contact lest they broke the spell too soon.

'Do you want me to go so you can get some rest?' She sat up, trying to cover her nakedness with the sheet they were both tangled in. Her skin was flushed, her hair mussed from their exertions and her eyes wide with either fear or uncertainty. This had shaken her as much as him.

If they were to stick to their agreement, there should be no cause for panic. They could take things at their own pace. There'd be plenty of time for him to over-analyse tonight's events when she was gone. All he wanted now was for his mind to be at peace with his body.

'There's no need to rush off. I can drop you off later. Unless you'd rather go?' He didn't know if she preferred to cut and run but, given the choice, he'd rather lie with her awhile longer.

'No, I… As long as it's okay with you?'

'I'm enjoying the company.' Rob patted the pillow beside him, so she lay back down and cushioned her soft curves against him. He sighed. It was nice to have something other than ghosts to share his bed.

'I don't usually do this.' She almost whispered the secret into his chest. As if they were doing something illicit.

'What? Sleep with colleagues? Hang around after

sex? Snuggle?' He buried his smile in her cloud of red hair. There was no way he was going to judge her for falling into bed with him when they'd both acted on the same impulse.

'All of the above. You're covering a lot of firsts for me.' She placed her hand on his chest and he could feel her relax against him again.

Her admission flashed up warning signs that this was moving somewhere Rob wasn't ready to go. In a lot of ways it was already too late. 'This is new to me too.'

His love life didn't usually extend beyond hotel rooms and the rare time he did bring someone home, he certainly didn't encourage them to stay. It already changed the dynamics when he already knew he'd be seeing this bed partner every day until the end of the month. They might as well enjoy this for what it was.

'Don't worry. I meant it when I said I wasn't in the market for anything serious. I've been there. Still have the wedding dress hanging in the closet.'

'We have so much in common.' Rob deliberately made her laugh. The split from her boyfriend had obviously been more serious than he'd first thought. Another good reason they'd established boundaries before taking things further. He was never going to be the man who could repair her heart when he was still trying to piece his own back together. Although he and Jessica were both officially single, it would seem they were still married to their pasts.

'So I can lie here without worrying you've got the wrong impression?' Jessica traced her finger around his nipple and reminded him of the real reason they were here. Sheer heat.

'I promise I have no plans for *us* beyond right now.' Rob grabbed hold of the hand teasing him back to full strength and rolled over to pin Jessica to the bed with both wrists.

She was wide-eyed and panting beneath him. 'Then we really shouldn't waste what little time we have left.'

The alien buzz of an alarm clock ripped Rob from the arms of the deepest slumber. Any other morning he was awake before it had the chance to blare out its air-raid warning of daylight approaching. He attempted to roll over and switch it off but he still had a naked Jessica sleeping on his chest. Enthusiastic lovemaking had apparently cured his insomnia. He would include that in the pro column for sleeping with her when the doubts started to creep in.

His first instinct should've been to shake her awake and get her out of here as soon as possible. Neither of them had intended for her to spend the night. He'd underestimated how much it would mean to have her in his bed when he wasn't in a hurry to put an end to the dream. He closed his eyes again. An extra five minutes wouldn't hurt.

'What time is it?' Jessica mumbled against his skin, lost somewhere beneath her mass of wild curls.

His nether regions began to stir, reacting to the novelty of a naked woman in the bed.

'Playtime?' He ran his hand along her spine and down to cup her butt cheek.

Jessica leaned over his chest to peer at the clock. 'As much as I'd love to, we both need to get to work.'

Rob nuzzled her neck and did his best to persuade her otherwise. Once they got up, the fantasy was over and they had to return to the real world. Coming back to an empty bed tonight was going to be even harder than usual.

Jessica curled around him, rubbing herself provocatively along his outer thighs, and plucking his nipple to attention. 'I don't have a change of clothes.'

'You really don't need any.' He palmed her breast, hungry for more than his porridge this morning.

'I think it might cause a bit of a stir if I turned up in last night's clothes.'

Rob wrenched his gaze from her rosy peaks to the rumpled clothes lying on a heap on his floor. 'You've got a point.'

There was also the reminder of her standing in his kitchen wearing *only* that shirt every time he saw her in it. It definitely wasn't work safe, for either of them.

'I have to go.' At least she said it with great reluctance as their one-night-only performance came to an end.

'I'll take you home. As soon as I'm wide awake.' Rob pulled the covers over their heads. He had no intention of leaving this bed until they'd said goodbye properly.

Jessica imagined all eyes were on her as she did the walk of shame through the doors, late for the first time ever. True to his word, Rob had given her a lift home. However, he'd also insisted on waiting for her. By the time she'd showered, succumbed to Rob's suggestion of one more 'last time' in the shower and changed, there was no way of her making it in time to work.

'I had to make a few follow-up calls,' she mumbled as she passed through the gallery. No one bothered to question her and, since she was the one always pulling overtime, she figured she was entitled to a bit of leeway.

The paperwork was piled up on her desk but her brain was mush. The perks of her position here meant she could position herself anywhere in the building without having to give a detailed explanation. She wanted time out to think over what had happened last night, and this morning. Everything else could wait. It was on her head if this project failed and she would pick up the slack when she was in a better frame of mind. A coffee and a seat in the waiting room would give her some space. The people in there were too preoccupied with their own problems to take hers under their notice.

Sleeping with Rob had been all she'd expected, and more. Their verbal contract that it was a one-time deal could do with a few amendments. The evening had meant so much to her on a personal level she was reluctant to end it there. More than the self-confidence she'd gained from how much Rob had wanted her, she'd also had fun. So consumed was she by her distrust of men, and her own insecurities, she'd forgotten what it was to simply have someone to laugh and spend time with. Since Rob had technically made the first move, it seemed they'd both abandoned their hang-ups in the heat of the moment and taken a giant leap forward. Unfortunately, if he was now primed and ready to move back onto the market, someone other than her was probably going to reap the benefits.

While she wanted him to crawl out from his well of sorrow into her arms, there was no way she could compete with the memory of his wife. A man like Rob was always going to want the whole package. That house was waiting for the wife who'd have dinner waiting on the table every night, and a tribe of overexcited kids to greet him at the door. She already hated the woman he was going to fall in love with.

It was her own fault for being greedy. She'd got what she wanted, only to find it wasn't enough. That one night would haunt her for ever—knowing she was so close to happiness, only for her useless body to spoil everything again.

She stepped into the lift and punched the button for the restaurant floor. If she was going to cry into her coffee, she deserved something that didn't taste like tar.

A thick forearm shot through the metal doors before they could close. She couldn't even have two minutes of self-pity without interference. Resisting the urge to keep pushing the button, she plastered on a smile for whoever was about to join her.

'Hi,' accompanied Rob's sudden appearance.

'Hi, yourself.' So full of angry thoughts at herself and a woman she'd never know, she kept her gaze firmly ahead. She didn't trust herself to act like a grown-up around him and pretend last night had never happened.

The lift doors closed and sealed her inside the steel box with Rob. She could sense his eyes on her as the lift whirred into life.

'I'm sorry if I made you late this morning.' As soon as he acknowledged what they'd been up to only a short time ago, all bets were off.

'It was worth it.' Jessica turned to meet his gaze and, in that instant, the heat was back. They flew at each other in a tangle of limbs and mouths, as if they'd never made it out of bed.

She gave an inward sigh as he pulled her close. This lapse wouldn't help untangle her thoughts about him but it was exactly where she wanted to be. With temperatures reaching critical levels, they broke apart.

'We shouldn't be doing this at work.' Rob took a step back and scrubbed his hands over his scalp, mussing his dark locks to give him back that bed-hair look. It wasn't helping to put last night out of her mind.

'Did you have somewhere else in mind?' They'd

seriously underestimated the difficulty they'd have keeping their hands off each other now they'd shared naked time together. If he was intent on imposing a restraining order on close body contact, he should really stop seeking her out. And find a different topic of conversation.

Rob coughed, trying to clear the cotton wool suddenly lodged in his throat. From the minute he'd left her at the hospital entrance that morning, he'd been craving another fix. Far from getting closure on this thing he had for her, their liaison had increased his appetite. Life had to go on, and he would do it one step at a time. So far, Jessica had made no demands on him. He was the one obsessed with commitment and the havoc it could cause.

'Last night. Could we do it again?' This concept was so alien to him he'd apparently lost the power of coherent sentences.

Jessica arched an eyebrow. 'What happened to your one-night rule?'

Sticky sweat moulded his shirt to his back as his comfort zone disappeared into the distance. 'We had a good time, didn't we?'

'Yes. Does this mean you want us to keep on seeing each other?'

'The next few weeks are going to be hell if I can't touch you after what we shared last night.' Even now, watching those amber flecks blazing to life in her eyes, he was fighting a losing battle with his libido.

'I did think you were being quite stingy with your idea of a fling. It should at least last as long as a girl is in town. Say, another two weeks?' Jessica moved closer and toyed with his top button.

He swallowed hard as it popped open at her behest,

replaying the moment last night when the spark between them had exploded into a fireball of lust. 'We'll have all the benefits of being in a relationship without any of the drama of trying to make it as a couple.'

'You want us to carry on seeing each other?'

'I thought since we had fun last night and neither of us wants a commitment, we could keep this going until you finish filming here. If you want?' It was the perfect set-up, as far as he could see. All the benefits of being in a relationship without any of the drama of trying to make it as a couple.

'You mean by day we'll be working together, acting every inch the professionals we are, and by night... horizontal deviants.' Jessica's wink as she approved his plan sent the temperature, and his pulse, soaring once more. Rob really needed this lift to hurry up before they were both sacked for gross misconduct.

'Yes, we'll need to make sure we keep our professional and personal lives separate from now on. No more of these clandestine meetings.' He was saying the words but as he dipped his head to claim her mouth again he knew he was becoming seriously addicted to the danger.

CHAPTER SEVEN

Rob resisted the urge to kiss Jessica when he met her in the car park. They were still technically on hospital grounds, which they'd deemed a no-go area since this afternoon.

They'd had a close call in the lift when the doors had opened mid-clinch to a group of elderly women who were thankfully too occupied with finding their car park ticket to notice. By conducting their affair at work, they were taking too great a risk of getting caught in a compromising position. Neither of them wanted to jeopardise their career for a fling which would be over before they changed the specials menu in the canteen. Instead, they'd reached the mature decision to wait until they'd clocked off before they dared touch each other again.

'I'm sorry if I've kept you hanging around all night. We had a new patient arrive with an aggressive stage three tumour, so we had to admit him straight away. In hindsight, I probably should've let you know so we could reschedule.' Timing was everything with these cases and cancer didn't take a night off simply because Rob had a beautiful woman waiting for him.

'Don't worry about it. I know you don't work a typical nine-to-five job. We were doing a follow-up with Cal and his family at home, so we've been off-site most of the day anyway.' Jessica's easy acceptance was probably because she worked similar fluid hours. That suited this no-strings arrangement but it also reiterated why it wouldn't work long-term between them. At some point he might want to settle down again and that would be next to impossible with two people who were slaves to their careers.

'How's he doing?' It wasn't often he got to find out about his patients in between hospital visits. Usually it was bad news if he saw them once they'd had the all-clear.

'Tired, but happy to be home. He had quite a fan club waiting to see him.' Jessica pulled out her mobile phone to show him a few photographs she'd taken of Cal with his mostly female friends.

'As long as he takes it easy.' He handed the phone back, his curiosity satisfied.

'Oh, he has an army of willing volunteers waiting on him hand and foot,' she said with a grin.

Now that Rob knew something of Jessica's background, he could understand the personal interest she was taking in the patient stories and how much their recovery meant to her as well as him.

He noticed Jessica shiver. Although the evening sun was shining, there was a definite nip in the air. Her floral strappy dress was pretty but scant protection from the Northern Irish weather.

'You're cold. We should get going.' There was no point freezing their bits off outside when they could be turning the heat up elsewhere. Preferably naked.

They made their way across the car park, the companionable silence punctuated by his growling stomach.

Jessica sniggered as they got into the car. 'I guess I'm not the only one who forgets to eat from time to time.'

'I hold my hands up to being foolish and missing lunch. Although, if memory serves, I was distracted on my way to the canteen this afternoon.' He leaned across to claim the prize he'd been waiting for all day. Unfortunately, as his mouth met Jessica's, his stomach protested again at being denied sustenance.

'You need food,' she murmured against his lips.

'I need you,' he insisted, deepening the kiss.

Another rumble.

'Right. That's it. We're making a pit stop for food on the way to your house.' Jessica resisted further overtures until he agreed.

'Okay. I'm sure we can manage that.' As long as it didn't interfere with their previously arranged plans, he was happy to grab some takeaway. He'd been reluctant to suggest dinner himself and take her to a more salubrious establishment in case it could be misconstrued as a date. They'd agreed to keep things purely physical to avoid any unpleasantness when it was time for Jessica to move on. Fast food was the perfect compromise.

'Good. You're going to need all the energy you can get.' There was a wicked glint in Jessica's eye, prompting Rob to get the engine started.

Tonight he had every reason to get home as soon as possible.

The steady rhythm of the car on the motorway played a lullaby for Jessica as she rested her head against the window and closed her eyes. Despite her best intentions, she was beginning to flag. They'd opted to sit in rather than take cold burgers and fries home and her full belly coupled with the long day was calling her towards sleep. Perhaps if she rested her eyes for five minutes she could recharge her batteries before the big night ahead.

'Jessica. We're here.'

'Mmm?' She heard Rob's voice calling her back to consciousness and struggled to open her eyes.

'You're home.'

When she was finally able to focus, it was to find they were parked outside her apartment block. 'What's going on?'

'You're clearly exhausted. We can do this another time.'

Jessica was wide awake at once. She'd promised him so much and let him down. 'Honestly, that was just a power nap. I'll jump in the shower, then I'm all yours.' She gave him her brightest, peppiest smile and prayed it was enough to convince him to stay.

Rob switched the engine off and she knew he was getting ready to see her off when he didn't take the keys out of the ignition.

'It's okay. I'm knackered too. Perhaps we overdid it last night. I think four times is a record for me and you can have too much of a good thing, you know.'

'Never. And, actually, it was five times, counting the shower. I think we were making up for lost time.' The thought that this wasn't a regular occurrence for him gave her some comfort. Not only did it mean she wasn't in competition with past lovers but that level of physical activity had clearly taken its toll. It would be impossible to repeat that on a nightly basis and function at work the morning after. Still, this wasn't the end to the evening she'd anticipated. She'd enjoyed having someone to talk to and lie next to as much as the sex.

'In that case, you've probably seen all my moves now anyway.'

'That doesn't necessarily mean I don't want to see them again soon. Won't you come inside with me?' She wouldn't beg him to stay, since that would make her look needy and fell outside the boundaries they'd drawn up. Although it would save her bruised ego if he did. Regardless of their pact, it was only human nature to be wanted for more than sex. Especially when even that had let her down in the past. What had there been to keep Adam when she'd lost interest in that too? Without children or passion, there'd been absolutely no reason for him to stay. They'd both known it. At least now she'd recovered part of what made her a woman, if not all of it.

'I'll see you to the door but I think we should call it a night before we burn ourselves out. We can pick up where we left off another time.' Rob had his seat belt off and was out of the car but there was no trace of anger or frustration at the change of plans. She wasn't used to a mature response in such circumstances.

'I guess I'll see you tomorrow, then.' She accepted her fate with a sigh as she rummaged in her bag for her keys on the doorstep.

''Night.' Rob leaned in and kissed her pouting lips.

It was amazing how revitalising one touch from this man could be, her body now fully alert. She dropped her bag so she could wrap her arms around his neck and pull him ever closer. Rob responded with two hands on her backside, turning this from a goodnight kiss to a lot more.

'We should take this inside before we really give the neighbours something to talk about.' She wasn't in the habit of snogging men on her doorstep and she could do without the inevitable 'Who's your boyfriend?' questions if they were spotted. There was no way of adequately explaining their arrangement to the well-meaning marrieds around here keen to see her partnered off too.

'I'm still not staying,' he mumbled stubbornly against the back of her neck as she opened the door. They practically fell into her ground floor apartment, giggling like a couple of teenagers. She was glad they seemed to have got their second wind, because she really didn't fancy a night on her own blaming herself for his absence.

'I'm going to grab that shower. You make yourself comfortable in the living room.' After a day trekking across the city for interviews, she wanted to freshen up. Stalling things for a little while might keep him here for longer than another fumble in her hallway too.

Rob groaned as she levered herself off him and headed towards the bathroom. 'Make it quick.'

She took longer than she normally would have under the lukewarm water for the simple reason she'd expected him to join her. Only when the temperature of the water dropped to gasping point did she admit defeat and turn off the shower. Teeth chattering and her skin turning a delicate shade of blue, she wrapped herself in a towel and went in search of her errant lover.

A quick check on her bedroom confirmed he wasn't lying naked on her bedclothes with a rose between his teeth either. He must've literally taken her at her word and stayed put in the living room. That would teach her to be coy about what she wanted in future.

Instead of the numerous romantic scenarios she'd envisaged of her man waiting for her, she found Rob had made himself a tad too comfortable.

'You've got to be kidding me.'

He'd left his jacket neatly folded over the arm of the chair, kicked off his shoes and was currently stretched out on her sofa, sleeping. She couldn't be cross with him when he looked so at home and so damn beautiful lying there. His lips parted on a soft snore, and the open top button of his charcoal-grey shirt was an invitation to get up close and personal.

She perched on the edge of the sofa and brushed a lock of hair from his face. His long dark eyelashes began to flutter as she touched him and she was almost sorry for disturbing him.

'Lie down with me,' he muttered without opening his eyes.

'My hair's still wet.'

'It'll dry.' He turned on his side to give her more room. Spooning was her weakness.

She snuggled in beside him. It was an age since she'd cuddled anything other than a cushion on this sofa. 'This is nice.'

'We don't have to do anything. I know you're tired.' Rob pulled the throw rug from the back of the sofa to cover them as he wrapped his arms around her.

'*I'm* the tired one?' She could already hear the change in his breathing as the past twenty-four hours caught up with him too.

'Shh. Go to sleep.' He buried his head against her neck and Jessica soon found herself following his command.

Rob wakened sometime in the early hours with a cramp in his leg and Jessica's hair in his face. It was far from an ideal place to sleep and yet there was a sense of peace lying here he was reluctant to abandon. With Jessica in his arms, there was no pain, or death or sorrow, only contentment. Unfortunately, her company was only a temporary solution to his problem and he suspected her departure would only serve to double his sense of loss.

The sound of birdsong outside burst the cosy bubble, signifying a new day and more firsts. It was unheard of for him to spend the night at a woman's home, never mind enjoy two consecutive evenings with the same one. By limiting liaisons to hotel rooms or a maximum of one night at his place, he maintained some control over proceedings. Those safety measures apparently went out of the window whenever he was with Jessica. This spontaneity was all well and good for a passionate affair but he hoped he wouldn't live to regret bending the rules for her. A sleepover at hers suggested a commitment he wasn't willing to give long-term.

Perhaps he could exercise some damage control by leaving before she woke. He shifted into an upright position and let Jessica fall back into his place. The blanket slipped onto the floor, leaving her in nothing but a skimpy towel. It would be so easy to simply tuck it back around her and walk away but he couldn't do that without coming off as a complete heel. At least if she wakened in her own bed it would show her he cared about her even if he couldn't stay.

He scooped her up into his arms and carried her to the bedroom, only her little moan against his chest indicating he'd disturbed her sleep. The towel came loose as he manoeuvred her under the covers and he made the decision to strip it away completely. It probably hadn't been the wisest move in the world to let her sleep in the wet fabric in the first place.

She was so serene lying there, scrubbed free of make-up with no glamorous clothes to hide behind. He understood why she dressed up even when she was so naturally beautiful. It was her way of protecting herself and covering her pain. She used cosmetics the way he used his position to maintain a certain distance from people but it must've been doubly difficult to keep the details of her illness hidden when she was usually so emotionally available.

He let out a yawn and checked his watch. There were still a few hours before he had to go to work. The bed looked a lot more appealing than the sofa. Jessica was naked. His shirt was damp from where she'd lain against him.

Suddenly he couldn't think of a single reason why he *shouldn't* strip off and climb in beside her.

'I thought you weren't staying.' Jessica curled into his side the second he joined her under the bed sheets.

'Temptation was just too great,' he said, running his hand over her shoulder and down to the curve of her waist.

Per their agreement, he didn't share the part about how she made him forget everything painful in his life when he was with her. He thought the first night he'd slept right through had been a fluke, simple exhaustion after their rigorous bedroom workout. Last night had challenged that perception. Fully clothed and in cramped conditions, he'd slept peacefully, free from nightmares and guilt. Jessica was the only common factor on both occasions. It would be telling if he noted any changes once he reverted to sleeping alone. Not that he was anxious to do that any time soon. Especially when there was a beautiful naked woman currently demanding his attention.

'How did we end up here, anyway?' The sheet slipped as she yawned and stretched, giving a tantalising glimpse of her full breasts. If she wasn't already snuggling back under the covers, he would've sworn she'd done it on purpose to make sure he didn't go anywhere.

Since they were both wide awake now with plenty of time to kill, it would be silly not to take advantage of the situation. He let his hand drift across her flat stomach and down towards her soft mound.

'I thought we might be more comfortable.' Although he was becoming anything but as his libido rose with the lark.

'And we're naked because...' She gasped as he slid a finger into her wet channel, and responded by raking her nails across his chest. It was an action he'd come to learn was a sign she was enjoying everything he was doing.

'I thought we might be more comfortable.'

'You're...so...thoughtful,' she said through panting breaths.

'I know.'

She was writhing against him, every stroke apparently bringing her closer to the brink. Rob threw the quilt over his head and burrowed down the bed, drawing a shriek of delight from Jessica.

He'd show her exactly how thoughtful he could be.

Two weeks into their fling and Rob still couldn't seem to get enough of Jessica. Even though they'd only parted a matter of hours ago at the hospital doors he was counting down the minutes until they could be alone again. She was a little ray of sunshine in the dark corridors every time she flitted past in her bright yellow outfit. A playsuit she'd called it and his thoughts were definitely playful when he caught sight of her long slim legs in the short all-in-one and strappy gold sandals.

He whistled the happy tune of a man secure in the

knowledge she was coming home with him at the end of the night.

'Someone's in a good mood.' Maria met him outside the door of the day unit.

'The sun is shining, I'm about to send one of my patients home…what's not to be happy about?'

'Hmm. It's just not…you. What's even weirder is I just passed Jessica humming that very same song.' She eyed him as if he'd been caught with his hand in the cookie jar.

'We must've been listening to the same radio station this morning.' It wasn't a lie. They'd both been rocking out to the same nineties music channel at the top of their voices in his car on the way to work. It turned out she was as bad a singer as he was, but equally enthusiastic.

'For goodness' sake, will you put me out of my misery and tell me you've finally made a move on her? Honestly, there's only so many meaningful glances a person can try to ignore.' Maria heaved a sigh as she waited for his confession.

His defences automatically shot up to protect his personal business from prying eyes, but Maria was his friend and invested far more than she should be in his love life. There seemed no point in denying it when he had nothing to be ashamed of.

'We're seeing each other but don't go buying a hat for the wedding. She's only here until the end of the month, remember?' Their relationship and this temporary high had an expiry date which would creep up on them before they knew it. He should mark out a chart or something to make sure he didn't forget.

'And what? You can drive from one side of this country to the other in a few hours. I'm sure you could still see her if you wanted.'

'I'm well aware of that but we've agreed this is for the best. You should be happy I'm having a bit of fun.'

Maria unfolded her arms and shrugged. It obviously wasn't what she wanted to hear but she was wise enough not to make another comment on the situation. They would never agree on what was best for him when she didn't know the circumstances which had brought him to Northern Ireland in the first place.

He followed her into the day unit and nodded hello to each of the patients receiving treatment. The oncology nurses were the ones who administered the chemotherapy drugs here once he'd devised the treatment plans. They were more than capable of removing the Hickman lines which were used for intravenous medicine and taking blood, when treatment ended. But he preferred to do this part himself when he could. That way he'd seen his patients through their illness from start to finish. It could be the most rewarding part of his job, performing this procedure when it meant the immediate threat to a child's life was over.

Maria was already in the cubicle with the ten-year-old girl and her mother waiting to be released from his care.

'I just need to check we have Katie Daniels, whose birthdate is the twenty-eighth of March here, in case I'm about to send the wrong person home?' He brought a nervous giggle from the child as she confirmed her details.

It wasn't until he went over her records again and saw those letters—ALL—he made the connection with Jessica. She would've been around the same age when acute lymphoblastic leukaemia had struck her too. He was eternally grateful for the fellow oncologist who'd saved her life. It proved to him how important his role here was for his patients and their families.

After he checked Katie's full blood count and clotting results were satisfactory he took off his wedding ring and gave his hands a thorough wash.

'Okay, Katie, I'm sure you'll be glad to know we're going to remove your Hickman line today.'

She bit her lip as she nodded but her mother's relief was more audible at having treatment come to an end.

'It's a relatively quick procedure. All you should feel are a few scratches when I numb the area around the line and some pressure as I remove it. You can stop me at any time if you're uncomfortable but it should all be over in a few minutes. Okay?' No matter how much he reassured her, it was only natural that she remained wary. He was glad when her mother reached over to take her hand to support her.

'I'm going to raise the head of the bed so you're more comfortable.' It also made it easier for him to access the site.

Maria stepped forward to lower Katie's hospital gown to expose her central line. Rob gently manipulated the tube so he could observe where the skin puckered and find the internal cuff holding it in place. He washed his hands again before donning sterile gloves and pulling a gown on over his blue scrubs.

He cleaned the area around the cuff carefully with copious amounts of disinfectant to create a sterile field and covered her chest with a sterile sheet, leaving just the site visible.

'I'm going to ask you to turn your head to the side and look at Mummy and so we keep the area clean we need to make sure you don't reach up and touch anything.

'Have you got anything planned to celebrate later?' he asked, trying to distract her from what he was doing.

'We're going to have a wee party at home,' Mrs Daniels replied as he drew up the local anaesthetic into the needle.

'My patients are always glad to see the back of me. I hope it's nothing personal.'

'You can come to my party if you want,' Katie said with her head still turned away as instructed.

'That's very sweet of you, Katie, but I'm happy just to know you're getting better. Now, you're going to feel those sharp scratches I told you about. If you want me to stop, you only have to call out.'

She nodded again and Rob could see her squeezing her mum's hand tighter.

He injected the anaesthetic in several areas around the cuff, careful not to hit the central line. Katie flinched when he broke the skin the first time but remained silent.

'I hope there'll be plenty of presents for you at this party too.' He stalled, waiting for the anaesthetic to take effect before he continued.

'I'm getting a puppy.' Katie's voice was positively shrill with excitement at the news. Although her mother was rolling her eyes at the idea, Rob knew from experience that the parents often promised their kids anything to help them through recovery.

'That's the best present ever. He'll be good company for you.' He lifted a scalpel from the tray Maria had provided beside him and made a small incision to release the cuff from her body. With stitch holders, he bluntly dissected the cuff until he could see the shiny white catheter.

'I need you to count to three and then I want you to hold your breath. One, two, three.' Rob applied pressure to the site and gently pulled the line free as Katie held her breath. It was important there was no air trapped in her chest, so he kept the pressure on her neck for a while after she started breathing normally again to make sure everything was sound.

'That wasn't so bad, was it?'

'Is it over?'

'As soon as we get you cleaned up.' When he was satisfied there were no complications, he cleaned the area again, closed the insertion site with Steri-Strips and covered it with a dressing.

'Can I go home now?'

'We need you to rest here for a little while, then you can go home and put all of this behind you.' There was no point hanging around reliving what had happened to her when she had the rest of her life to look forward to. The irony of that sentiment wasn't lost to him as he pulled off his gloves and retrieved his wedding ring from the sink.

'Maria will keep an eye on you until you're ready to leave. Watch out for any tenderness or discharge around the wound over the next few days, but that's us finished.'

'Thank you, Doctor, for everything.'

'You're very welcome.' He shook hands with the grateful mother, his wedding band mocking him every time it caught the light.

As soon as he was out of the ward, he wrenched it off his finger to study it. It hadn't occurred to him to take it off in five years and he knew Jessica would never expect him to do it for her either. The more he stared at it, the more he thought it was tying him to the past. Whilst he was wearing it, he was still half of a couple which no longer existed.

In the eyes of the world he was unattached; indeed nothing in his actions indicated he was still a married man. He certainly wouldn't be sleeping with Jessica if that was the case. The ring was nothing more than his security blanket now, his way to keep people at a distance. Except for the next couple of weeks at least, he wanted Jessica as close as possible.

Before he changed his mind, he pulled out his wallet and slipped the ring in beside the precious family photograph he kept there. As tough as it was to admit it, the only way his heart could heal was to let Leah and Mollie go. He would always carry them with him but that didn't mean they were still here. It was time to move forward without them.

Jessica turned the pasta down to a simmer and stirred crème fraiche, chilli flakes and tomato and basil sauce into the chopped peppers and tender-stem broccoli in the pan. The chicken breasts were in the oven and the table was set for two. She wasn't sure she could call this a celebratory two-week anniversary dinner considering it meant they were already halfway through their time together but at least someone was finally making use of Rob's fancy kitchen.

When it had become obvious he wouldn't be leaving with her, he'd insisted on ordering her a taxi and handed her the keys to his house. They both wanted to spend what was left of the evening together.

She'd made a detour to grab the makings of dinner and throw a few of her things into an overnight bag. It would save a lot of hassle in the morning when they'd invariably end up running late. The pressure was off now they'd established the nature of their relationship, so they could stop pretending she had any intention of going home.

She heard his car pull up outside as she assembled her ingredients into one spicy dish.

'Something smells nice.' Rob slid his arms around her waist and nuzzled into her neck.

It took great effort not to respond to his touch when she'd been waiting for it all day but she didn't want all of her effort to go to waste if they gave in to their hunger for each other. 'I thought it was about time someone christened this cooker.'

'How very domesticated of you.'

'Don't panic. I'm not marking my territory or anything. I thought we could both do with a proper sit-down meal.' She quite enjoyed cooking but it always seemed a terrible waste of time doing it for one.

'I'm not complaining. You're welcome here any time.'

If only that were true and there wasn't a deadline looming. She was getting used to this idea of domestic bliss and they were altogether too comfortable together, in and out of the bedroom, for this to remain a meaningless fling. She knew it but she didn't care. It was too late to retreat now when the damage was already done. The idea of no longer being with him was too hideous to contemplate and she was in this deeper than she'd ever imagined possible. All she could do now was enjoy the ride while it lasted. There was no other option but to walk away at the end of filming or she'd end up reliving that nightmare of rejection. Her appetite seemed to disappear with every mouthful.

After dinner they moved over to the sofa, where she'd grown accustomed to cuddling into Rob's chest at the end of a hard-working day.

'One of my patients finished treatment today,' he said with obvious relief.

'That's wonderful news.' Until he'd come into her life she'd forgotten the good parts of being part of a couple—sharing their stories and letting the stresses of the day ebb away in each other's embrace. It was a simple act which could be taken for granted when there was someone to come to every night but one which would be greatly missed in an empty house. There was only a fortnight left of playing the happy couple, then it was back to reality.

'How was your day?'

'Not as good as yours, I'm afraid. We had some technical issues with the remote cameras, so we've lost today's outside footage. We'll have some continuity dif-ficulties to iron out in the edits.' It was a headache she didn't need but one she was sure they'd overcome. She wasn't one to give up without a fight.

'My poor Jess.' He dropped a kiss on her forehead and she felt better already.

She threaded her fingers through his, her heart al-most stopping when she found the groove where his wedding ring once resided. There were any number of reasons why he might've removed it. Perhaps he'd forgotten to put it back on after washing his hands or caught it on a door handle and mangled it out of shape. Maybe he'd accidentally sewn it inside a patient. Any-thing seemed more plausible than removing it because of her but she couldn't bring herself to ask him about it.

The significance of that last scenario would scare her to death and force her to finish this earlier than expected.

A change of clothes and a toothbrush no longer seemed like the biggest step in their relationship.

CHAPTER EIGHT

JESSICA STOPPED BY the noticeboard in the corridor as one of the fundraisers took a red marker to the scanner appeal barometer.

'Every little counts,' she said, colouring in a few extra squares to take the total to almost three-quarters of the way to their target.

'Hopefully, exposure from the documentary series will boost it even more.' Jessica wanted the filming to benefit the patients and families as well as tell their stories.

'Fingers crossed.'

Once the wielder of the felt pen walked away, Jessica studied the pictures pinned to the board, charting the progress of the fundraising. They'd held bake sales, car washes and charity auctions—with Rob playing a part in every one. His dedication to the cause was admirable and completely justified now she'd met so many of the children herself. They were also the reason she was here and she never wanted to lose sight of that. After the events of the past weeks, there was a definite possibility of that happening.

She and Rob had made each other late again this morning but she couldn't complain. That reckless passion was more in keeping with a sizzling, no-strings fling than getting cozy on the sofa every night. The let's-talk-about-our-day level of intimacy was a different story, a one-way ticket to heartbreak. At the end of the day, someone like Rob needed someone more than her. She should never forget that.

'We still have a long way to go.'

For a second she thought she'd imagined Rob's voice until he cast a shadow over her.

'What? Oh, yeah, the scanner. I'm sure you'll get there.' *See, your focus is totally screwed. You thought he was talking about you.*

'Are you signing up?' He tapped on the latest money-raising idea pinned to the board.

'A fun run? Me?' It was a daytime event but in which context did he expect her to attend? Friend? Lover? Colleague? If she declined, she sucked as a human being in every category.

'It'll probably end up as more of a sponsored walk but it'll still be fun. We're taking the trail in Tollymore Forest Park in County Down, hoping to make a day of it. You're welcome to join us.'

'Next Saturday? I'll have to see if I can arrange a crew to cover it.'

'Actually, I think I'd prefer if they weren't there.' Rob ruled out the easiest option for her to justify being there by taking away her safety net.

He was close enough for her to see that he hadn't had time to shave this morning. The sight of his stubble and the memory of it grazing against her skin as they made each other late for work reminded her why it was dangerous for them to be alone together. She shivered in his shadow.

'We'll see' was all she would commit to for now.

'These might help make up your mind for you. I

forgot to give them to you last night.' He produced a gift bag from behind his back and a wave of panic washed over her.

'You didn't have to do that.' She had avoided the present-giving stage of relationships for a long time and took the bag between thumb and forefinger as though she'd somehow catch commitment from it. *That way madness lies.* At least that was what she told herself when she had only her mother to exchange gifts with over birthdays and major holidays.

'I know. Just open it.'

She held the package at arm's length while she opened it in case it exploded into a confetti of hearts and flowers. It was too heavy for jewellery or chocolates, and not tall enough for a wine bottle. A peek inside found a pair of trainers nestled in pink crêpe paper.

'What the hell…?' She pulled out a shoe in case the surprise was stuffed inside, but no, this was the actual gift he couldn't wait to give her.

'I can't stand seeing you in pain at the end of the night, after hobbling around in those heels all day. You should give your feet a rest every now and then.' He took the glittery pink footwear from her to display it in his hand with his best game show host flair.

'Thank you.' One pair of trainers bought with the welfare of her feet in mind suddenly became the most thoughtful gift in the world. And the scariest. Things were progressing too quickly to remain casual but she didn't want to quit him.

'And now you have an excuse to wear them.' He looked so pleased with himself, Jessica couldn't disappoint him by refusing them.

As she watched him walk away, she only wished

she had something more than long working hours and
a dodgy medical history to offer him in return.

Despite her reservations, the glitzy footwear brought a
smile to Jessica's face every time she donned them. At
least the children approved of them, even if she'd received a few curious glances from her colleagues who
were used to seeing her in more formal attire. A week's
worth of shoe-focused attention was preferable to breaking in new trainers on a five-kilometre run and limp-
ing her way towards the finish line. That bit of forward
planning ensured she was comfy in her own shoes as
she started this race. At least, as comfortable as she
could be standing in the middle of a forest dressed in
a tutu.

She caught Rob sneaking another sideways glance
at her.

'What?'

'I'm still surprised you dressed up and I definitely
thought you'd be more of a glamorous princess than
a sparkly fairy.' He shook his head as he assessed her
choice of costume.

Jessica gave him a twirl so he got the full effect of
her shimmering wings outside the confines of his car.
She liked the fact that she could still surprise him even
when they were virtually spending twenty-four hours
together.

'Ball gowns and glass slippers aren't conducive to a
hike in the country. Silver leggings, trainers and a pink
tutu are much more suitable.' Today was about having fun and raising money; it wasn't a fashion contest.

'It's not like you to be practical.' He raised a dark
eyebrow as he eyed her outfit again.

'I can do comfort when it's called for. I guess all of

that advice isn't completely wasted on me after all.' She tapped him on the head with her starry wand and danced ahead of him in the queue for their race numbers.

'Perhaps I should have worn the same?' He did a little shoe shuffle to show off the neon-pink leg warmers to go along with his eighties-themed outfit. Only the rucksack on his back, packed with medical supplies for emergencies, spoiled the look.

'I think you're rocking the Day-Glo singlet and Bermuda shorts perfectly well.' If he'd gone for the authentic tight white shorts, her heart might not have survived. She was having trouble enough not staring at his bulging biceps, never mind other protruding body parts.

'And I nearly forgot this—' He pulled a white headband from his bag to complete his ensemble and proved beyond doubt he had a sense of humour beneath the serious facade.

A lot of the staff had taken time over their costumes but there were a few whose ideas of fancy dress were based on novelty T-shirts. Jessica was glad Rob wasn't afraid to show off his fun side in public. It made him all the more endearing. As if healing sick children and catching fainting women wasn't enough.

They gave their names at the makeshift running station in the car park and received their numbers and route maps in return.

'You've got quite a turnout,' she remarked as they joined scores of people at the starting line.

'I recognise a lot of the faces too. There's a few of my old patients here with their families.' Rob grinned and waved over to everyone who caught his eye. It was obvious how delighted he was that they were far enough along in their recovery to take part. His big heart was one of the reasons she loved him.

She could try to fool herself that it wasn't true but all the signs were there. Why else would she spend every waking moment thinking about him and could no longer imagine sleeping anywhere but in his arms? Every layer she'd uncovered had made her fall harder and faster for Dr Robert Campbell.

The revelation was so great Jessica found herself sprinting away from it when they fired the starting pistol. She'd done the one thing she'd sworn not to and fallen in love. Now there was no way of getting out of this with her heart intact. Even if there was the slightest chance he could return the sentiment, there were too many hurdles for them to overcome. They would only be postponing the inevitable if they tried.

Twigs snapped beneath her feet as she tore up the ground in her bid to outrun the injustice of it all. She'd found someone who truly made her happy, someone she could be herself with, but there was still that skeleton lurking in her closet which would ultimately drive him away.

Before she could devise an escape plan, the object of her misplaced affection was speeding to her side.

'Hey, wait for me.'

'Sorry. My competitive instinct took over for a minute.' She slowed to a more realistic pace for a woman more chocolate bunny than gym bunny—one which didn't threaten to explode her lungs. Unfortunately, the deceleration didn't help regulate her thumping heart.

'Trust me, you're going to need to save that energy for the finish.' He gave her a wink and sped ahead, demonstrating his own competitive streak.

The track thinned out alongside a rocky stream, forcing them into single file and ending conversation between them. It gave her a chance to think about the consequences of her errant emotions, as well as ogle his backside.

She'd deliberately prevented him from staying at her house since that night to avoid this very situation. As if virtually moving into his would make any difference. In theory, setting time parameters was supposed to counteract such complications. In reality, feelings trumped everything.

Okay, so they travelled together to and from work when schedules allowed and they spent every night in bed together, but she hadn't planned this. What she did know was that he had permeated into every aspect of her life and it was going to be a Herculean task to remove all traces of him when she was expected to move on. Rob was part of her working day, as a doctor and confidante. At night, he was her companion and lover. And she didn't want to lose him in either capacity. This was exactly why she shouldn't have got attached from the start. They'd let emotion creep in where it had no business being, by nosing into each other's pasts.

Until this project began she hadn't entertained the idea of getting serious with another man. Adam had shattered her confidence and the belief that she could ever be enough for any man. Rob had showed her otherwise. At least on the surface. Now she was wondering if there was a way she could make this work with Rob. They were both single career people who so clearly enjoyed each other's company.

Although he was very good with the children, he hadn't made mention of a desire to have any of his own. It was entirely possible that Jessica had projected her insecurities onto him, making excuses for this relationship not to succeed beyond the length of the documentary shoot. For all she knew, he had issues of his own in that department. Perhaps he'd buried the idea of a family with his wife. Perhaps she should stop jumping ahead to the idea of marriage and children when he'd promised her nothing more than a few weeks in his bed. Even if they carried on, the spark between them could very well fizzle out before it reached the stage where it mattered.

There were only two ways she could see to deal with this serious breach of her heart and neither would necessarily end well for her. Either she could keep this new information to herself and pretend the end of the affair wouldn't crush her, or confess. Whilst she'd keep her fingers crossed that he could be prompted into declaring his undying love for her too, the likelier scenario was another rejection. He hadn't asked her to fall in love with him, never expressed an interest in extending their fling into an *actual* relationship. But if this was her last chance at having someone to grow old with, she would never forgive herself for walking away without a fight. Though he didn't know it, Rob held the key to her future happiness—a burden he might not be ready, or willing, to accept.

This new development in their courtship would change the dynamics between them for good. If she decided to share the news with him.

As the trail opened out again onto the forest floor, the throng of runners fanned out to create a colourful spectacle amongst the trees. The laughter and chatter of the group was a happy sound to behold, unless you were struggling to hear the decisions your subconscious was telling you to make. With a desire to be alone with her thoughts, she fell back from the crowd. She slowed to a walking pace and it wasn't long before Rob noticed.

'What's wrong, slowcoach? Are you admitting defeat already?' He was running back towards her, a vision in neon emerging from the dark woods. *Fit* in every sense of the word.

For fear of having to explain her sudden lack of commitment to the run, she doubled over and feigned injury. 'I think I've got a stitch.'

It wasn't a complete lie—there was definitely a sharp pain stabbing her insides that made her want to curl up into a ball. His face was a mask of concern as he jogged to her side, multiplying her level of guilt in the process.

'Take a few deep breaths and try to walk it off.' He fell too easily for the fib, enabling Jessica to keep the pretence going for a little while longer.

She straightened up with a grimace, making all the right groaning noises as she did so. Rob retrieved a water bottle from his backpack and instructed her to take a sip while they walked.

Whether it was a fake running injury or fainting from hunger, he was always there to catch her. Given his caring nature, he would probably show the same level of care for anyone in need, but he wasn't sharing his bed with them at night. Jessica had discovered for herself it wasn't so easy to keep love and lust separate at all times.

Her inner optimist held out hope that Rob's compassion would extend to all areas of her health problems. So he would understand her fertility issues, accept them and love her regardless. She was asking for the world.

Rob kept a close eye on Jessica as they made their way deeper into the forest towards the babbling stream. She was quieter than usual and he didn't think it was merely down to a stitch in her side. He'd seen her bounce back from worse than that. It wasn't like her to separate herself from the rest of the group either. Usually she would be right where he should be too—in the thick of things, keeping morale up. Not watching as the others disappeared into the trees. The imposed solitude hinted that she wanted to be alone with him for a reason and he wasn't about to complain. They'd grown so insular, cooped up at his place, it was nice to spend time together outdoors for a change.

With the documentary series beginning to wrap up Rob knew they were on borrowed time but he wasn't ready to say goodbye just yet. If there was a way they could keep on seeing each other when it ended, he would jump at the chance. He couldn't, didn't want to replace Leah and Mollie, but he couldn't stand the thought of losing Jessica either. Was five years of denying himself happiness punishment enough for his guilt, or should it remain a life sentence? Everyone else thought he'd been too harsh on himself but they weren't privy to all the facts. Jessica was the one person in whom he might be able to finally confide the truth. Her reaction would tell if he'd sufficiently served his time and they could see where this thing led them. He didn't want to throw away what he had with Jessica because he was afraid of being happy without Leah and Mollie.

He took the lead as they reached the crossing point of the river to scout out any hidden danger first. Although it wasn't necessary as Jessica skipped across the stepping stones after him like a woodland nymph. She was a shimmering light in the murky shadows of his world and he didn't want to be plunged back into darkness again once she was gone.

'Is everything okay?' he asked, holding out a hand to help her take the final leap.

'I'm feeling much better. Thank you, Doctor.' She fluttered her glittery eyelashes at him as she joined him on the riverbank and Rob couldn't resist moving in for a kiss.

Their lips met under the dappled shadows of the trees. The gentle swish of leaves in the breeze and the steady trickle of the stream serenaded them and created the perfect idyll for them to be together.

'I wish we could stay here for ever,' he whispered into her hair as he held her tight. He hadn't meant to say the words outside of his head but she didn't flinch at the sentiment. Everything seemed so easy here in each other's arms with nobody else to think about.

'Me too.' Her wistful sigh kept the dream alive as they rocked together for a little while longer.

Rob caught a flash of movement in the trees across the stream and the spell was broken. 'I think we have company.'

'It was too good to last,' Jessica tutted as a band of latecomers burst onto the scene in high spirits and full voice, disturbing the tranquillity. He hoped it was only the peace and quiet she was talking about.

'Come on. We can try to keep a few steps ahead of them.' He grabbed her hand and started back on the trail in the vale of the Mourne Mountains. If he was going to spill his deepest, darkest secrets, it would be somewhere without an audience.

Jessica giggled as they power-walked away from company like naughty schoolchildren caught playing truant. 'What happened to the affable doctor with time and a friendly word for everyone?'

'Even he needs a timeout now and then. Perhaps he's finally taking notice of those people telling him he should get a life of his own.' For the time being, that included Jessica and he intended to make every second count. That included days off and fun runs.

His partner in crime squeezed his hand in what he hoped was solidarity. Should he follow that advice to the letter, he very much wanted Jessica to be a part of that new start.

They circled round the duck pond and, once they were sure they were far enough ahead of the rest of the party, they came to rest on a bench. Jessica stretched out her legs and tossed her head back. Rob envied the sun as she gave herself to it without hesitation. He didn't know where he stood with her and he was sure she was still holding something back from him. Time with her had shown him he could still love his family and have feelings for her too. If he could get her to commit to something more than they had, he'd like to explore what that meant.

With his head in a whirl, he left her and walked down to the water's edge. He swung his backpack around and rummaged inside until he found what he was looking for. The ducks had always been a highlight of the trail for him and he never came empty-handed. Armed with a handful of oats, he knelt down to draw them closer.

'I'm sure Scottish wildlife love their porridge but I'm pretty sure the ducks around here prefer good old-fashioned bread.'

Rob shook his head. 'There's no nutritional value for them in it. In fact, it can cause bloating and generally damage their health. Not to mention the uneaten bread lying about which affects the water quality and attracts vermin. You're much better feeding them oats, corn or even grapes cut in half.'

'You've done your homework.' Jessica joined him, holding her hand out for duck bribes too.

'This was always Mollie's favourite part.' The words slipped out before he had time to think about it but even saying his daughter's name aloud parted the clouds of sorrow keeping her hidden from the world. It had been too long since he'd said it. To go from calling it out every day to avoiding any mention of her was as hard to accept as never seeing her sweet face again. He was thankful for one more chance to give her a voice. Regardless of his mistakes, she deserved to be remembered.

Her name hung in the air, waiting for Jessica to retrieve it.

'Mollie?' Jessica carried on chucking lunch out onto the water, oblivious to the significance of Rob's reminiscing. He was entrusting her with the memory of his daughter, the most precious thing in his life.

He closed his eyes and took a deep breath.

'It wasn't only Leah I lost in the accident that day. I had a little girl too.' It was as if he'd opened a valve, releasing all the pressure of his grief which had been building up inside him for so long.

He was starting to learn that remaining stagnant wasn't doing him any favours. Losing Mollie was the most traumatic event in his life and he'd tried so hard to bury it. As though it was something shameful. He wanted so desperately to believe he could trust Jessica with her memory.

Jessica gasped, inhaling the breath he'd just let go of. 'Oh, my God! No! I can't... I don't...'

It was a lot of information to dump on her and he understood how overwhelming the information was. What could you say to someone who'd lost a child? What could possibly make any difference?

He'd heard it all.

'At least she's with her mother.'

'She's in a better place.'

Every trite comment made him want to punch something. She was still his daughter and he'd lost her for ever. The enormity of that could never be expressed sufficiently. Perhaps it was better that Jessica said nothing, rather than trot out another meaningless cliché.

'How old was she?' Jessica's eyes filled with tears as they spoke and Rob was forced to turn away. It was a simple question; he hadn't expected it to cause him to well up more than he already had. There was no turning back now.

'Four. I have a picture here.' He fished in his back pocket for his wallet and the worn family photo he kept in it. There were no photographs in his house because he wanted to avoid awkward questions and his guilt. However, he'd kept this one close to his heart for the past five years. The small reminder of everything he'd lost when they started to fade in his thoughts.

'Is this Leah too? They're both beautiful. You all look very happy together.' Jessica's reaction held no trace of jealousy or exasperation as she was presented with his previous life. Rob was grasping at the idea that he'd found someone with room in her heart for all three of them.

'We were. Most of the time.' He tucked the photograph back where it came from, wishing he could hide his feelings just as easily.

'Why didn't you tell me?' Jessica's voice was a soft whisper invading his memories.

'This was supposed to be a no-frills deal, right?' He gave a humourless laugh. *'I killed my wife and daughter'* definitely didn't fall into line with that frivolous idea of fun she'd been looking for.

'I know, but we've shared so much these past three weeks. What made you think I couldn't handle knowing about your daughter?' The frown creasing her forehead and the defensive body language said she was hurt by his omission.

It was going to be difficult not to make this the 'It's not you, it's me' line.

He swallowed the ball of nerves lodged in his throat. He delivered life-altering news every day of his career but none which could potentially impact on his own as much as this. The real reason he'd kept Mollie a secret was to hide his shame at failing her. He didn't think he could bear it if Jessica turned her back on him once she learned the truth but he couldn't live a lie any longer. They wouldn't stand a chance at a future together unless she knew the *real* Rob Campbell.

'I didn't tell you everything about the accident. No one knows the full story. Which is why people are happy to paint me as the victim when I'm the one to blame. I told you about the row Leah and I had the night before the accident. We'd argued about Mollie's childcare. Leah was a model before she got pregnant and she'd started taking on assignments and dragging Mollie along with her without telling me. I thought our daughter deserved more attention. How much of a hypocrite does that make me for staying at home when I should have been with them, shopping for my little girl's first day at school? You can't imagine having to live with the knowledge that you sent your own wife and child to their deaths. I let them both down.' He sank down onto his knees. All that remained now was the shell of a man who'd once been a husband and father.

Jessica sat down cross-legged beside him, paying no attention to the mud clinging to her pink chiffon skirt, and took his hand in hers. He'd never fully appreciated the importance of hand-holding before now. She was showing him she was there for him, reminding him he wasn't alone.

'I still stand by the fact it wasn't your fault, regardless of any argument or that your daughter was there too. Surely your family can see that?'

'I never told them. I couldn't live with everyone knowing the truth and hating me as much as I hated myself. It was easier for me to just pack up and leave.' A decision he'd questioned at various points over the years but he'd left it too long to try to build bridges with his family now.

'Rob!'

Jessica nearly sent him sprawling into the dirt as she slapped his arm.

'What was that for?'

'You've spent so long beating yourself up I didn't think one more dig would hurt you. Seriously, though, five years cut off from friends and family is more than enough punishment for something that wasn't your fault. They didn't do anything to deserve that, did they?'

'No. I just couldn't cope with everyone telling me how I *should* be feeling, what I *should* be doing. I couldn't hear my own thoughts above theirs any more.' He'd been treading water on his own for years.

'Haven't you had enough space by now? What if you had been in that car? You might've been killed too. And what of the lives you've saved over these past years too? Do they mean nothing? You've accomplished so much in your career, made a difference to so many people. Isn't it time to reconnect with those who care about you?'

'I hurt them. Some of the things I said... I don't even know if they'd want me back.' He'd been hurt, angry, and he'd pushed away the few people he'd had left in his life. He'd packed up and walked away to start afresh. Except he hadn't. All he'd done was lock himself away with his grief in another country.

'Of course they will. They lost Leah and Mollie, and they lost you too. I'm sure a phone call would put their fears to rest.'

He'd never considered his parents', or Leah's parents' loss. The light had gone out in everyone's lives when they'd died. At the funeral and during the days following, all he'd been able to think about was the two white coffins and his own pain sealed inside. Leah's parents might have lost their daughter, but his parents had lost their son too. He'd been selfish and it took someone with Jessica's guts to point that out to him.

'We'll see. One thing at a time.' He was learning to deal with the here and now first.

'I think it would do you good to have someone here for you.' Jessica's understanding was the reason he'd finally shared Mollie with her. They'd come a long way since she'd come barging into his department and he'd wanted to show her and the film crew the exit. Now she was the one he wanted to be here for him.

'You asked me why I hadn't told you. The truth is, I've never trusted *anyone* enough with the full story. I don't want people thinking I can't do my job objectively because of what happened to me. It's private.

I've learned to be very selective about my friends over the years.'

'I would suggest "selective" to the point of friend, singular.'

'Look at it as your privilege, and not my madness.' He relaxed into a grin. After everything he'd told her, she was still here. Every time he'd imagined telling someone about losing his daughter through his thoughtless actions, he'd pictured them running away as fast as their legs could carry them. Not sitting here telling him to pull himself together.

'I'm not sure what I've done to deserve such an honour but I'll accept it if it means you'll stop living in the past.'

That serving of tough love had stopped Rob from falling further into self-pity. He hadn't considered anyone other than himself in his actions and he could see it was time to let other people in to share his life. He was edging ever closer to making a commitment to something other than his grief.

'Okay, okay, I get it. No more moping. You can be a hard-ass when you want to be, Jessica Halliday.' He'd already started to think more about his future over these past days and he was hoping she would be a part of it. With her help, he might just be able to free himself from some of the guilt weighing him down.

'I do have a certain reputation to maintain. As honoured as I am that you've shared all of this with me, I am curious why you've decided to tell me now.' She was almost daring him to say how he felt about her.

'I know we agreed to end things when filming finished but now that it's approaching it seems foolish to set a time limit on what we have. We're good together, Jessica.' He stopped short of saying those three little words before he scared her off altogether. The next great reveal could wait until he knew there was a possibility she could love him back.

She didn't disagree but she was glad when the stragglers caught up and interrupted their conversation. This wasn't the time to reveal how she felt about him with people milling around feeding the ducks and taking refreshments. Especially when she was still trying to untangle the mess of emotions Rob had tied up even tighter in the past ten minutes.

The tension she'd sensed between them hadn't been leading up to Rob declaring his undying love for her, as she'd imagined. He'd given her something even more precious. Confiding in her about Mollie meant more than those three words, which didn't always turn out to be true. It was right up there with removing his wedding ring. Her pulse started to quicken as the implications set in. It was so much to take in.

He was telling her he wanted to be with her, something her heart ached for too. But her love could never be enough to replace everything he'd lost. Fate had cruelly struck her for a second time. Despite all her precautions, she'd fallen head over glittery running shoes for Rob and she was still going to have to end it. She couldn't take another rejection, which would inevitably follow once he heard about her infertility. This was a man who needed another family, deserved one, and she could never give it to him. It would be better for her in the long run if they stuck to the original agreement instead of dragging this out to the messy, painful finale. She wouldn't lead him on and let him think she was the special woman he'd been waiting for.

He'd held on to that loss for so long it was evident

how greatly it had affected him. The void in his life was as great as the one in hers for the child she would never have. Rob couldn't possibly find closure with her. How dare she expect him to move on from the past with her when she couldn't give him a future to look forward to. Her heart was aching, the pain of losing him tearing her apart inside, but she couldn't show him that. He shouldn't have to take on the responsibility of her pain when he'd made it clear from the start he wasn't ready for a relationship. It was her fault she'd let things get this far.

Adam had been right. She could never sustain anything meaningful without the resentment of her infertility coming between them.

'We should get moving before they send a search party out for us.' She got up and dusted herself down, ready to move on. She was good at that.

Rob scrabbled to his feet beside her. 'Thanks for hearing me out. I promise I'll think about contacting my folks.'

'Good.' Then the onus wouldn't be entirely on her to love and support him when she would inevitably let him down.

'We'll finish the rest of the discussion in private,' he said for her ears only. Apparently it didn't matter to her body that she'd already ended the relationship in her head as that growly Scottish promise brought goosebumps to her skin. This was going to have to be a clean break, with no lapses into his arms if she hoped to survive.

'Later,' she promised, although she planned something a lot less intimate than he probably had in mind. This break-up speech would serve her better when she was dressed in more sombre clothes, on neutral territory and preferably somewhere she could walk away from.

She steeled herself to tackle the rest of the run and was grateful that the last leg of their journey was mainly uphill. At least he wouldn't expect her to talk when she was gasping for breath.

CHAPTER NINE

ROB WAS FINALLY making peace with the past. After coming clean with Jessica he'd gone home and made that call to his parents. It had been a long, emotional reunion over the phone but one they'd all needed. The result of it was another weight lifted from him and an invitation to Belfast for them. They didn't believe he was to blame for what had happened any more than Jessica did. All they wanted was for him to be happy. And he would be as soon as he and Jessica found time for their heart-to-heart.

Now he was free to build a life after Leah and Mollie, he couldn't wait to take the next step with his feisty redhead. Unfortunately, the universe seemed to be conspiring against him getting anywhere close to her these days.

The fun run, coupled with the emotional baggage he'd unloaded onto her, had understandably left her drained on Saturday night. He'd agreed to the suggestion they spend the weekend apart for her to recover and take everything on board. But this was now Tuesday and paranoia was beginning to set in.

Logic said her busy schedule was to blame for the rushed phone calls and his quiet nights without her. These were the last days of filming and he knew she was trying to get everything wrapped up. It was the timing which made him antsy. He was trying not to link her sudden coolness to him spilling his guts about Mollie and the row he'd had with Leah before the crash. Jessica had been so understanding and supportive; he couldn't imagine she was now taking umbrage over it. The only other subject they'd touched on before she went AWOL was their relationship and he'd expect her to tell him straight if she wasn't interested in him any more. She'd never been behind the door in saying how she felt about anything since they'd met.

Time was running out and he'd wasted enough of it denying himself happiness. He intended to bring this to a head today so they both knew exactly where they stood before they let something good slip away. The best way to do that without interfering too much with her work was to combine the two. He'd scheduled that one-on-one interview she'd been so keen to get on tape from day one, so she had no more excuses not to see him.

Sitting here in a glorified storeroom with a camera pointing at him might have appeared an excessive way to get her attention but Jessica was worth it. He'd spent long enough with his life on hold and he would do whatever it took to ensure they had a future together.

Jessica bustled into the room a good five minutes later than they'd agreed, her arms full of papers and a coffee in her hand. 'I'm sorry I'm late. I won't keep you too long.'

He could've been any random off the street waiting to do a vox pop for all the interest she showed in him. There was no eye contact, no sly smile, no indication at all that they'd spent the majority of the past month in his bed. He frowned at the lack of familiarity even when they were the only two people in the cramped room. A matter of days ago they wouldn't have been able to keep their hands off one another and he didn't know what had happened to change that.

'No problem. It's just us, then?'

'Yes. Everything's set up, ready to go. I have enough technical experience to shoot these interviews myself with a static camera. It makes them more—'

'Intimate?'

'I was going to say relaxed, but I guess that works too. Basically, I'll ask you a few questions relating to your job and if you could answer directly to the camera it would be great.' She ignored the blush he'd brought to her cheeks and the reason for it as she maintained her professional stance in the face of his provocation.

'I get it. Then you'll edit out your questions so it looks as though I'm talking to myself?'

'I prefer to see it as a monologue to the camera, to the viewers who want to hear your personal experiences. Now, are you miked up?'

It crossed his mind to pretend otherwise and have her rummaging under his clothes with the microphone pack in the vain hope the contact would reignite the fire between them. In the end he decided against it, since she seemed keen to keep a camera between them at all times. 'Yes. I'm ready to roll when you are.'

He understood she had a job to do and this project was important to her. It was the only reason he was going along with this. For now.

Jessica willed her hands to stop shaking and prayed Rob couldn't see them. In hindsight, coffee probably hadn't been the best idea for her jittery nerves as she watched it spill over her notes. She wasn't looking forward to the conversation she had to have with him once the professional one was out of the way. She'd been deliberately avoiding it and the realisation she'd fallen hopelessly in love with him since the fun run. Hopeless when there was no possibility she could give him the type of fulfilment he deserved in life.

She'd justified the white lies she'd used to stay out of his bed as a way to create distance so the final blow wouldn't be completely unexpected. In reality she'd been too chicken to end things face-to-face. She was worried she would cave in at the last minute, afraid he'd see through her lies but most of all terrified he'd find out the truth and reject her anyway. Now they were here, alone, and she knew there'd be no more running away from him. As soon as she got what she needed from him.

She cleared her throat and took a sip of coffee, relying on the caffeine to see her through this without collapsing into a heap of jelly. 'Okay, we'll need an introduction. If you could just tell us your name, your role here and what your day-to-day routine is, it would be a good start.'

The irony of what she was asking wasn't lost on her. She knew everything about him, more than most people in his life. Rob had shared his most intimate secrets with her and she was pretending his life was a complete mystery to her for the sake of the camera. Worse, she was treating him like a stranger to protect her heart, with no thought for his. She salved her soul with the knowledge he'd survived a greater trauma than the premature end of a fling.

Once the camera was rolling Rob sat up straight to deliver his piece. He was making this easier for her than she'd anticipated. So far he'd followed her lead and swerved any mention of their relationship, or questioned her absence since Saturday. The insecure jilted woman inside her took it as a slight, ridiculous given the circumstances, but deep down she still wanted him to fight for her. Every closet romantic needed to believe they were worth loving even if it was a doomed venture.

'I'm Dr Rob Campbell and I'm the consultant paediatric oncologist at Belfast Community Children's Hospital. I treat young cancer patients and coordinate their care with a team of radiotherapy and surgical specialists. My job is to make sure each child receives the best possible care from the moment of diagnosis. This includes administering chemotherapy and deciding which combination of treatments will be most effective for the individual. I also liaise with the families to keep them informed at every stage of their child's treatment.'

His position here sounded straightforward when it was broken down into simple terms. The director had made the right call asking for more personal footage of Rob. Snippets of him in between patient stories could never adequately convey his emotional commitment to everyone who came through those hospital doors. At least the footage they had with the Girl Guides would show the rapport he had with children, whether they were patients or not. He'd probably been a fantastic father and she was sure he would be again some day.

She blinked away the tears burning her eyes to find he was staring at her, awaiting further instruction.

'That's great. Now, could you explain to the audience what chemotherapy actually is and what effect it has on cancer cells?'

He gave her a questioning glance as if to say *You know better than anyone what chemo is*, but this wasn't about her. Besides, they could use his definitive explanation to narrate any relevant segments involving chemo treatment.

'Sure. Chemotherapy is the name given to the drugs we use to kill cancer cells. These can be given as tablets, liquids or as injections into the bloodstream, muscle or spinal fluid. The drugs are then absorbed into the bloodstream and carried around the body to reach and destroy cancer cells.'

She appreciated that he didn't dwell on the inevitable side effects when normal, healthy cells were also damaged. They would be obvious on the faces of all those they featured over the course of the series. Unless you were extremely unlucky, those side effects subsided when treatment finished.

'Tell us why an MRI scanner is so important to the department.' Her promise to promote the appeal was the main reason he'd agreed to be interviewed, so she attempted to sweeten the blow coming by giving him what he wanted.

Rob leaned forward in the chair, his forearms resting on his knees and his steely stare directed down the camera as he prepared to do business. Shivers played along Jessica's spine. She knew how it felt to be the focus of his intense passion and her life was going to be colder without it. Without him.

'At present, we are the only specialist children's hospital in the UK without an MRI scanner. Unlike other procedures, an MRI scan is less invasive and exposes the patient to less radiation. Any child who requires a scan currently has to be transferred to the adult hospital, with some even forced to travel outside the country to receive one. An in-house scanner would cut waiting lists, diagnose patients quicker, and scans would take place in a familiar environment. The scanner will be completely funded by volunteers and we still have a long way to go to reach our target. We've undertaken bake sales, fun runs and all manner of sponsored events to raise money. These children deserve the very best healthcare we can provide, so all donations are welcome. Every penny counts.'

If Rob's impassioned plea didn't get the general public to open their wallets, nothing would. She'd be sure to play it to her contacts too. There were several she knew who made considerable donations to charity every year to ease their consciences about the extravagant lifestyles they led.

'I'll make sure we put all of the details up at the end of each programme, so people can donate straight to the fund.' Something more than bittersweet memories should come out of her time here.

'Thank you.' He was addressing her directly for the first time since they'd started the interview and she was grateful for the static camera when her hands began to tremble again. Every minute she spent here with him told her what a wonderful man he was and how much she would miss him. She had to get through this as quickly and efficiently as she could—wrap up the relationship along with the production and edit the highlights to air at a later date.

'We're on to the last couple of questions now. I know you have a lot of people to see.'

'I'll always make time for you, Jessica. Whatever you need, you only have to ask and I'll do everything in my power to give it you.'

She couldn't listen to those sorts of promises. They'd failed her once too often.

'All I need is five more minutes,' she said, deliberately misunderstanding his intentions.

Rob sighed and sat back in his chair. 'Then you have them.'

Jessica experienced another surge of disappointed relief when he conceded so easily. Perhaps the devastation of the break-up would be more one-sided than she'd imagined. She was the one who was going to have trouble getting over this for a long time. In some ways it could be harder to pick herself up after Rob than it had been with Adam. He'd gradually chipped away at all the defences she'd built since her doomed engagement. Until she was here, vulnerable, hurting and with no way out but to end the best thing she'd had in her life for as long as she could remember.

'Okay, back to the day job. What would you say is the best part of what you do here?' The faces of Max and Cal immediately popped into her head and the fantastic characters of the children she'd met in such a short space of time. There were definitely good memories to take away from here as well as the unhappy ones.

Rob's serious expression gave way to his beautiful smile. 'My favourite part of the job is definitely meeting all the characters on the ward. Despite what they're going through, the children always brighten my day. We do have a lot of fun in between the treatments. Undoubtedly, when I'm able to tell families their child's cancer is in remission it's a relief for me as much as them. I'm here to make them better and that's the outcome we all strive for. Oncology can also be an exciting field as we further our research and participate in new clinical trials. An estimated seventy-five to eighty per cent of children now survive cancer, thanks to the work that's being done.'

'And the most difficult part of the job?' They both knew what that was. She hated having to make him go to that dark place but she needed the viewers to hear it and feel it from him. Not all of the patients would be as lucky as her. Lauren's poor family had been able to take her home but in less happy circumstances.

'The worst part is having to deliver bad news to the family. Having to tell a parent their child's illness is incurable is something that stays with you for a long time. You're effectively handing down a life sentence when you say the treatment isn't working. I know what it's like to be on the receiving end of that sort of conversation. My four-year-old daughter died in a car accident, so I'm able to empathise a great deal with the families in those circumstances.'

Jessica paused filming until she was sure he was ready to share Mollie with the rest of the world. 'You don't have to—'

'I want to. No more secrets.' He waited until the camera was rolling before he spoke again. 'Losing a child is the hardest thing a parent can go through. It's only possible to get through it with the love and support of those around you. I wouldn't wish the pain I went through on anyone, which is why I'll do everything I can to prevent other families suffering. There isn't a day goes past when I don't think about Mollie.'

Jessica's vision blurred with tears when his voice cracked on his daughter's name. This was such a huge step Rob was taking by confronting his past so publicly. She was sorry she couldn't see it through to the end with him. He was moving forward but she'd remain frozen in time for ever. The only future she had now was her professional one.

She swiped the tears away with the back of her hand. 'Thanks. I think I've got everything I need now.'

Those blue eyes stared back at her from the other side of the camera. They seemed to reach deep into her soul and see her lies.

* * *

'Have you? What about us?' Rob couldn't understand the sudden drop in temperature between them. It seemed the more he opened up, the further Jessica withdrew. If he'd completely misread the bond they'd developed these past weeks together, he wanted to hear it from her.

'We had fun. That's all it was ever supposed to be.' She casually packed up her things as if what they'd shared meant nothing to her. Rob knew that wasn't true. Their relationship had stopped being casual when she'd stayed the night in his bed.

No longer content to sit and wait for her to validate their relationship, he got up from his chair and went to her. 'That's how it started but we both know it's a lot more than that now. These last days without waking up next to you have been hell. After losing Leah and Mollie, I never thought I would want anyone in my life again but you've made me realise that's exactly what I want. Maybe I'm wrong but I kinda got the impression you were happy being with me too.'

'I was but it's over, Rob. The job's done and so are we. I'm glad you're in a better place and I wish you all the best but I can't be part of this new life.' She turned and reached for the door handle but he couldn't let her leave until he knew why. He placed his hand on top of hers in a plea for her to stay.

'Talk to me, Jessica. One minute we're inseparable and the next you're waving me on my way as though we were nothing more than a holiday romance. Tell me what's changed between us since Saturday. I'm sorry if I overwhelmed you by pouring my heart out about Mollie but I needed to do it to give us a chance. All I'm asking is that you do the same. I know we're nowhere near the stage of discussing marriage and babies yet but at least I'm starting to see there's a future waiting for me out there. I really want you to be—'

'I can't do this.' Tears were streaming down Jessica's face as she shook him off and ran out of the door.

Rob didn't go after her when she clearly needed time out from him. He didn't know what he'd done to upset her except say how much he cared about her. If she truly didn't reciprocate those feelings, there would be no need for such an emotional reaction. There was pain in her eyes, sorrow in those tears, and he wanted to understand what was behind it. For the life of him, he couldn't fathom why she was causing them both unnecessary hurt. Perhaps he'd been too wrapped up in his own problems to see she had her own. Jessica had helped him exorcise his demons and he'd be there for her too if she'd let him.

They had something worth fighting for and he wasn't prepared to give up without finding out what was troubling her. If this was one of his cases at work, he would step back, assess the situation, find the source of the problem and treat it. He wouldn't accept the end until all possibilities had been exhausted.

CHAPTER TEN

THE THUMPING ON the front door threatened to drag Jessica back to consciousness. She stuck her head back under the pillows and waited for it to stop. After the agonies of the day, all she wanted was to fall back into oblivion and forget everything.

Her desolate womb had cost her another chance at happiness. Even for Rob, the man she thought could love her, flaws and all, her infertility would've been a deal-breaker. Right up until today she'd held on to that scrap of hope that he'd take her in his arms and tell her it didn't matter. In the end, she hadn't needed to mention it. He'd made it clear how important having children again would be to him and left her in no doubt about where she stood—on the outside, looking in at Rob while he played happy families with someone else.

She sandwiched her face between the mattress and the pillows and let her tears fall. With any luck, she'd simply drown in her own misery instead of having to go through this again.

There was more knocking. Louder. She lifted the pillow so she could call out.

'I'm not in!'

Whoever it was should really take the hint she wasn't welcoming visitors today.

They didn't.

'For goodness' sake!' She was forced to throw the covers back and get out of bed to confront the orchestrator of her unwanted alarm call if she was to stand any chance of sleep. Reluctant to be parted from the only source of comfort available to her, Jessica shuffled to the front door with her duvet still wrapped around her body. She yanked the door open, ready to let rip at whoever it was disturbing her already fitful sleep, only to find a persistent Scottish doctor on her step.

'I don't want to talk.' She instinctively tried to slam the door shut so she wouldn't be forced to have the conversation she'd done her best to avoid so far.

Rob wedged his foot inside. 'Well, I do. So stop being so bloody selfish and let me in.'

He wouldn't budge, leaving them in a ridiculous stand-off, made all the more absurd with Jessica cocooned in her bedcovers. She gave in with a loud huff and grudgingly granted him permission to cross her threshold.

Her mood wasn't further improved by how much better he looked coming off the late shift than she did. Bar some extra rugged stubble and his now wrinkled blue shirt, he was as handsome as ever. She, on the other hand, probably had mad bed hair, panda eyes, and was wearing her Super Sloth duvet cape.

'I'll keep this simple. There's no future for us. As a couple, I mean. We still have a future, separately, with work, and, you know, breathing and stuff.' She was rambling now but she hadn't expected to see him again. He'd turned up right in the middle of her grieving process and set her back even further.

Walking out on him had already left a crater in her heart the size of the Giant's Causeway. A void which no amount of casual affairs could ever fill. In some ways not having Rob in her life would be harder to come to terms with than no children. He wasn't making it any easier for her by being here when she'd made the decision to walk away from him.

'I don't believe you.' His you-know-you-want-me huskiness made her catch her breath.

No. No. No. It wouldn't do to give in to her weakness for him when she was already at an all-time low.

'Believe what you like. We're over.'

Anyone would think this guy had never been dumped before. Looking at that magnificent physique filling her eyeline, she could see why he probably hadn't. His refusal to let this matter go was simply prolonging her agony. All she was asking for was space to grieve this relationship so she could move on. Something he'd needed once too and an impossibility when he insisted on reminding her of what she was missing.

'I don't get to have a say?'

'This isn't about your ego. If it makes you feel any better, you can tell people you called it off.' Jessica was a cornered cat, hissing and scratching trying to protect herself. She needed him out of her life, not close enough for her to feel his warmth and smell his aftershave.

'I just want to know why.'

'I'm sorry but, trust me, I'm saving us both from a lot more heartbreak further down the line.' If he would only trust her judgement on this and let her go, he could find the woman who could give him everything he needed. And she could get back to something she had a chance of succeeding at.

'Do you have a crystal ball? Unless you've developed psychic powers, you have no idea how things might pan out. You can't tell me you don't want this.' He pulled her close with one arm around her waist and kissed her hard. His mouth crushed hers and he held her tight so she couldn't get away.

This was her chance to deny him, prove she was immune. She tightened her lips into a line of resistance, but Rob didn't stand down. He merely changed tactics. The hand restricting her movement now rested on the small of her back, the pressure on her lips eased as he skirted along her defence line.

She parted her lips for one more memory to cling to. As she lost herself in one last dizzying kiss, the rasp of his stubble on her skin vaguely registered. All she was doing now was opening up old wounds simply to satisfy her craving.

She turned her face away. 'If you're quite finished—'

Rob gripped her chin in his fingers and forced her to look at him. 'I love you, Jessica.'

She swore her heart screamed, *No!*

The words every girl wanted to hear made her want to run. There was no air in the room. She couldn't breathe.

First came love, second came possible marriage, third came a disappointed fiancé and a broken-hearted shell of a woman.

No, thanks. Been there, done that, got the tear-stained T-shirt.

'You might think you do, Rob, but really I'm nothing more than your rebound girl, your link back to the real world with whom you're mistaking lust for something more. You think you need to justify a sex life by concocting a fairy-tale romance to accompany it. Well, you don't need it. We're both consenting adults. You don't need anyone's permission to live your life the way you want.' *Ugh.* She hated herself for patronising him so much but she couldn't get sucked into this delusion for her own sake. A happy-ever-after was never going to be within her grasp.

'I know our relationship this far hasn't included talking about our feelings for each other but I'm leaving myself naked here. I'm being honest and I wish you would do the same. Look me in the eye and tell me you don't love me.'

'I'm sorry, but I don't feel the same.' The cruel lie burned her throat as it made its way to her lips.

Rob's face scrunched into a mask of hurt. 'Say it.'

'I don't love you.'

She confirmed her place in hell by denying the truth for a second time. Rob had gone through so much to get to this point and Jessica knew he would never have said those words to her on a whim. He *thought* he loved her but that was only because she hadn't been straight with him. To someone whose entire family had been wiped out, losing the chance to have another would matter some day. It was better to finish this now before she was in too deep.

'No? I would be more inclined to believe you if there weren't tears in your eyes.' Rob cradled her face in his hands so tenderly they fell all the more easily.

'I'm tired. Someone interrupted my sleep.'

'And I'll let you get back to bed as soon as you tell me the truth.'

'I don't love you,' she whispered, closing her eyes so she wouldn't have to look at him.

He brushed her tears and lies away with the pads of his thumbs. 'I'm pretty sure crying when you're dumping me invalidates that argument. For the record, you're a terrible actress. Forget saying those words if that's what's freaking you out but I don't see why we can't keep on seeing each other. I know you'll be moving on to the next job but it's not as if we live at opposite ends of the country. Why throw something good away?'

She snapped her eyes open, forced to defend her actions. 'We want different things. It would never work.'

'What? One of us wants to sit around brooding over her deadbeat ex, and the other wants to seize another chance at happiness?'

'You're not being fair.'

Neither was she and the truth was the only way guaranteed to get him to back off.

'I can't have children, okay? We both know that's a deal-breaker. Cancer and early menopause have pretty much ensured I will never be able to give you that replacement family you so desperately need.'

The great burden of her secret lifted from her shoulders to Rob's. She no longer had to fight her way free as his arms fell to his sides and he let her go without a word.

There was no jubilation to be had from her verbal victory. All she'd done was prove her point. When it came down to matters of the heart, she was no use to anyone.

It took a moment for Rob to come to terms with the reason she'd been holding back. Of course he knew infertility was a possible side effect of prolonged and intensive chemotherapy but Jessica was such a force of nature he never thought of her as a cancer victim. She'd been doubly unlucky. If she'd been older when treatment had started, they could've taken steps to freeze her eggs so she would've still had the chance to be a mother one day.

'I'm so sorry, Jessica.' He'd been here a hundred

times, offering sympathy to those whose lives had been destroyed by cancer and the words always seemed so inadequate.

Wrapped up in her comfort blanket, she looked very much the frightened child who'd probably gone through hell in those early years, but she'd come through it. Rob didn't want her to ever be sorry she had, simply because it had cost her the chance to have children. Perhaps he'd been *too* open about the effect losing Mollie had had on him. It would be easy to interpret that as a desperate need to have another child but that wasn't where his head was at right now.

'Yeah, well, there you go. The truth is out there. Don't let the door hit you on the way out.' She dropped her comforter and adopted her warrior pose—arms folded, lips pursed and defying him to love her.

'Why would that make a difference to how I feel about you? Do you really think I'm so shallow that I would stop loving you because of something you can't give me? What about everything you have given me— friendship, understanding...love?' He'd really messed up if she thought all he wanted was to replace Mollie. Jessica had given him so much by simply being there for him and he'd failed to do the same for her.

'I've been through this before, remember? I know how it ends. I've spent the last four years picking up the pieces after the last guy I broke that news to. You have permission to go back on the market with a clear conscience. I don't expect you to hang around and pretend we have a future when you have the pick of the fertile bunch out there. I'm sure there'll be no end of broody women lining up to make chubby-cheeked babies with you.'

Clearly he wasn't the only one having trouble letting

go of the past. It hadn't occurred to him that the walls around her heart were even taller than his.

'Do you remember the conversation we had about me hating people telling me how I should feel and how I should act? Yeah, that. I don't want anyone else but you.'

'You say that now but when it comes down to it—' She bit her lip and he could see the pain she was trying to keep at bay.

'I'll be there.' He needed her to believe in him, and herself.

'I'm such a catch. Remember, on top of my inability to conceive, there's the double whammy that the cancer could always come back again. I wouldn't inflict that on you when you've been through so much already.' She seemed determined to put him off by putting up more imaginary barriers but she'd forgotten she was the one who'd taught him to live in the here and now.

'I'd always had you down as a glass half full kind of girl, not glass half full of vinegar. Neither of us can base our futures on what-ifs. You're here, you're healthy, and that's all that matters.' And he loved her. If he was to take his own advice and stop focusing on the negatives in his life, he had to face up to the fact he was in love with a beautiful, smart woman who meant the world to him.

'But I can't have kids. That won't ever change.'

'Aren't you jumping the gun here? I only asked that we could keep seeing each other.' He managed to coax a wry smile from her. They both knew he wanted more than that.

'I know. I'm simply thinking ahead.'

'I'm not saying I wouldn't love to be a father again some day but if it doesn't happen, it doesn't happen. If the time comes when we would want a family, there are other options available. I would be more distraught at the thought of not having you in my life. When Leah and Mollie died, I went with them. For five years I've led a zombie-like existence. I was nothing more than an animated corpse cursed with life, forced to go through the motions of the daily grind. Then you came along and showed me what it was to love again. I can live without any more children but I can't live without you, Jessica.' He reached out and took her shaking hand in his. It wasn't only Jessica who was afraid of rejection. He wasn't sure if this—or he—was enough.

'Just so you know, if you turn me down again I'm going home to lock myself in a dark room with a family-size bar of chocolate. If I go into a sugar coma, it will be entirely your fault.'

'No pressure, then?'

'No pressure.' He was trying to keep the atmosphere light, since there was a danger of one, or both, of them dissolving into a snivelling mess. Given the burning in his throat and the moisture gathering in his eyes, there was every chance he would crack first. He couldn't lose her.

Maybe it was because she was in her comfort zone, maybe she was tired and emotional, or perhaps Rob Campbell was too damn understanding, but Jessica was starting to believe this could happen. If he really didn't think her infertility was an issue, it seemed only her insecurity was keeping them apart. She loved him, he loved her, but she was scared of leaving herself open again.

'Seriously, how can this ever work, Rob? We've got more baggage between us than the luggage department at Debenhams.'

Rob's hearty chuckle did more to warm Jessica than

her fifteen-tog duvet had. 'True, but who else would have us?'

'A family man without a family and a feeble, barren excuse for a woman. You're right. If we put that on a dating site, we'd be lucky to get a hit.'

'Ahem. *Feeble* is not a word I would ever use to describe you. *Stubborn*, *pig-headed*, *temperamental*, *compassionate* and *beautiful*, perhaps.' He stroked his thumb across her fingers. The tenderness coming from such a big man always surprised her. He'd never once portrayed the oaf which should have accompanied his height and build.

It was only one of the many things she loved about him. It was her own fear which stopped her from admitting it.

'Thank you.' Words could never fully express her astonishment that he still wanted to be with her despite everything she'd told him.

'You're wrong about one thing, though. I do have a family.'

'I know you do. I meant one of your own.' Tact wasn't one of her best qualities but he'd mentioned his parents so infrequently in the time she'd known him, she'd forgotten they existed.

'Thanks to you, I got back in touch with them last week. They want to meet up.'

'That's fantastic. I'm so pleased for you.' It would be good for him to spend time with his family. They had a lot to talk over and he might finally get some closure. She had a strange ache to be a part of that.

'I've told them about us and they want to meet you too.'

This was huge. Now there were no more excuses. She had to decide if she was going to take the leap of faith with Rob, or play it safe. As scary as it sounded to be someone's other half again, she owed it to herself to try.

She swallowed hard. 'I'd love to.'

'Say that again,' Rob demanded.

'I said, I'd love to meet your parents.'

'Oh. Sorry, I thought you'd finally admitted you loved me.' He wasn't that good an actor that she was convinced he'd misheard her.

She hadn't actually revealed that piece of vital information to him yet and she wasn't inclined to give it away so easily. 'Nope. I definitely said I would love to spend time with your parents.'

'Try again.' He pulled her into his arms and whispered into her ear, sending shivers tiptoeing across the back of her neck.

This time there was no denying how she felt about him. 'I love you.'

'Good, because I love you too.' Rob dipped his head and covered her lips with his. The kiss was a promise that everything was going to be all right.

Jessica had finally found her cure.

EPILOGUE

'IT'S TIME.' JESSICA gave Rob a gentle shake beside her. She was propped up against the headboard of the bed, trying to relieve the back pain, but it was getting to the point where she would soon need his help. There'd been something special in the quiet time between her contractions, knowing the child she'd thought she'd never have was on the way, but Rob wouldn't have wanted to miss a second of this.

'Uh-huh,' he mumbled into his pillow, still half asleep. With all the running around he'd been doing lately, he was bound to be exhausted. On top of his day job, he'd been attending prenatal classes with her and decorating the nursery. Not to mention all of the cooking and cleaning duties he'd undertaken since she'd started waddling into the final weeks of pregnancy.

She loved this man so much it hurt. Literally.

Another contraction started to take hold, tightening her belly and stealing her breath away. She squeezed her eyes shut and waited for it to pass.

'Jessica?'

She could hear her husband scrabbling to sit up beside her and the flick of a light switch as he finally came to. Once the pain began to subside she opened her eyes again to see his panic-stricken face staring back. 'The baby's coming.'

Rob leaped out of bed, clad only in a pair of black jersey shorts, and did a circuit of the room. 'Okay. Your bag's packed, we have your birth plan, I've got the hospital on speed dial…let's go.'

He was making her dizzy, pacing up and down the sidelines with the intensity of an athletics coach at a race meet. Any minute now he'd pull out a stopwatch and time her contractions, pushing her to beat her personal best.

'We've got plenty of time yet. I'm going to run a bath, have a cup of tea and relax as much as I can.' The contractions were far enough apart for her to indulge. There was no point heading to the delivery ward until labour had progressed further.

'Do you want me to phone the guys?' The way he said it left her in no doubt that having a camera crew here was the last thing he wanted. Her too. Since the success of the initial documentary series and the follow-up piece on getting the MRI scanner at the hospital, she'd started charting their road on IVF too. There were so many people going through the same process she thought it was important to record the trials and tribulations along the way. Rob had been supportive thus far but even she knew where to draw the line.

'They can wait. This is our time.' She didn't want to share it with anyone other than her husband.

'Good. I'll put this in the car and phone the hospital to let them know we'll be coming in.' Rob pulled on a pair of jeans and grabbed the overnight bag Jessica had ready to go.

He paused by the door and turned to look at her

with the biggest smile spread across his face. 'This is really happening?'

'Yes. It's happening. As soon as you help your pregnant wife out of bed.' Jessica swung her legs around to the edge of the bed and with Rob's assistance heaved herself up into a standing position.

'You need to take it easy.' He frowned as she took a few steps towards the bathroom.

'I think I can manage turning the bath taps on without coming to too much harm.' She shrugged off his concerns and shooed him out of the way. For someone who'd spent so long fighting her own battles she was still trying to come to terms with having a partner who looked after her so well. He'd been so attentive from the second they saw those two precious blue lines on the pregnancy test, Jessica knew their baby was going to feel as loved as she did.

These past two years with Rob had been the best of her life. He'd changed her from a relationship-wary, hardened singleton into a gushing romantic. Every day with him was filled with love and confirmation she'd made the right move in taking that leap of faith with him.

Things had progressed quickly between them once she'd finally admitted her feelings for him and let go of her fear. Meeting his parents had been emotional for all involved but they had welcomed her and Rob both into their lives. Talking everything through with them seemed to have finally brought him some closure and he'd proposed to Jessica within six months. By that stage she had no qualms whatsoever about the depth of his love for her and vice versa. After wasting so much time locked in the past they'd both been keen to marry quickly and make the most of what life had to offer.

Now they were about to have the happy ending they both deserved.

Rob insisted on making the tea whilst she walked the halls of what was about to become their family home, trying to ease the pain in her lower back. She managed only a few sips before she was forced to abandon it. Within seconds she was doubled over and squeezing Rob's fingers until they turned blue as another contraction took hold.

'Are you okay?' He waited until she'd stopped crushing his hand before asking. She could tell he was only moments away from bundling her into the car, regardless of her protests. This was definitely the anxious husband and soon-to-be father heading into the delivery room with her rather than the logical doctor. In some ways it was comforting to know he was still as overwhelmed by the situation as she was even though he wasn't a first-time dad.

'Just uncomfortable. I think I might climb into that bath now.' She hobbled back towards the bathroom with her Rob shadow trailing behind her to find her bubble bath lit by candlelight.

'I thought it would help keep you relaxed.' Rob unnecessarily justified his own thoughtfulness as she kissed him on the cheek.

'Thank you but I draw the line at whale song in case you were thinking about it. It's a bit too close to home under the circumstances.' As if to prove her point, she was forced to ask him to help her struggle out of her nightie and into the water. She'd loved every aspect of being pregnant but she would be glad when she could see her feet again.

'You're beautiful,' he said, kneeling at the side of the bath. Every time he said it she believed him a little more.

'Do you think the person who donated her eggs re-alises how much she's given us?' Jessica stroked her bump, rising out of the bubbles like an island in the mist. After revealing her deepest, darkest secret to Rob he'd recommended counselling for her to come to terms with her fertility issues. It was during these sessions she was reminded she still had options.

Things had deteriorated so badly between her and Adam that she'd never explored other avenues. They never would've survived the process they'd gone through to get here today. Her bond with Rob had been strong enough for them to face all the hurdles together.

Since marrying Rob the urge to have his baby had become all-consuming. They'd considered adoption but when it was explained to her there was still a chance of her carrying Rob's biological child herself she'd been determined to see it through. He'd been worried the complicated process of IVF and donor eggs would prove too stressful for her but this was one time the odds had worked in her favour. The donor eggs, fertilised with Rob's sperm in a lab, had been successfully implanted in her womb first time around.

'Whoever it was deserves to be as happy as we are. This is everything.' Rob rested his hand gently on her belly and leaned over to kiss her.

Here with her husband, waiting for the arrival of their baby, Jessica no longer saw herself as a victim. She was one of life's winners.

Rob felt Jessica's abdomen tighten at the same time as she flinched away from him. He hated seeing her in pain and if he could've gone through this for her, he would have. She'd been so strong and determined this far, he knew it would be worth it in the end when they were holding their baby.

He held her hand as she panted through another contraction. 'Okay, water babies. They're getting closer. I think it's time to think about getting out.'

Jessica's grimace eventually softened into a grin at the same time the circulation came back in his fingers. 'I think Junior's of the same opinion.'

Rob grabbed a towel and helped her out of the tub. It didn't matter how relaxed she was about the birth, or the fact he was a qualified doctor, he would be relieved when they got to the hospital. There were so many possible complications in pregnancy, not to mention her chequered medical history, she would be safer in that environment than a remote house in the middle of the countryside.

'If he's as strong-minded as his mother, he'll be here in no time.'

'*He?* Do you know something I don't?'

'A figure of speech, I assure you, but Junior does lend itself to the possibility of a son…' He was teasing her. They'd decided against finding out the sex, having been blessed with this chance to complete their family. Rob didn't care if they were having a boy or girl as long as mother and baby were healthy.

'Hmm. We'll see. *She* could be as reluctant to join the outside world as her father had been.' As usual, Jessica parried back. Marriage certainly hadn't snuffed out that spark between them. There was never a dull moment with her in his life and he often wondered how he'd survived on his own for so long.

He'd never imagined he'd be given the chance to have this again and he would cherish every moment he had with Jessica and the baby.

'Er…Rob?'

It took only a second for him to register the shock in her eyes and the puddle of water between her feet and what it meant. 'Your waters have broken?'

'Yes.' For the first time since she'd woken him there was a hint of panic in her voice. Unsurprising when his own stomach was flip-flopping with anticipation of their imminent arrival.

'Okay. We got this.' It was affirmation to himself as well as Jessica that, come what may, they would get through these next hours together.

Jessica was lost in those blue eyes. Every struggle in her life had been worth it to get to this perfect moment.

'He's beautiful,' Rob whispered, his voice cracking as he stroked his son's head.

'He takes after his daddy.' With the mop of dark hair and brilliant blue eyes, he was definitely Rob's mini-me.

'Given the short time it took him to get here, I would say he has his mother's determination too.' Rob smiled and dropped a kiss on her forehead.

He'd held her hand the whole way through without flinching, even during the sweary, shouty stage of her labour. Thankfully, it had been a relatively straightforward delivery, so quick there hadn't been time for any pain relief other than the gas and air. At least it meant she was fully compos mentis to enjoy every second of this miracle.

'I can't believe he's really ours.' She might not be his genetic parent but after carrying him for nine months she was every inch his mother.

'We'll need to get used to it soon. The three of us are going to be together for a long time.'

Jessica watched as he cradled their baby in his arms,

smiling and cooing and totally besotted. She counted herself very lucky indeed. Rob had healed her heart and now, with a family of her own, she finally felt complete.

* * * * *

MILLS & BOON®
Hardback – January 2016

ROMANCE

MILLS & BOON®
Large Print – January 2016

ROMANCE

The Greek Commands His Mistress	Lynne Graham
A Pawn in the Playboy's Game	Cathy Williams
Bound to the Warrior King	Maisey Yates
Her Nine Month Confession	Kim Lawrence
Traded to the Desert Sheikh	Caitlin Crews
A Bride Worth Millions	Chantelle Shaw
Vows of Revenge	Dani Collins
Reunited by a Baby Secret	Michelle Douglas
A Wedding for the Greek Tycoon	Rebecca Winters
Beauty & Her Billionaire Boss	Barbara Wallace
Newborn on Her Doorstep	Ellie Darkins

HISTORICAL

Marriage Made in Shame	Sophia James
Tarnished, Tempted and Tamed	Mary Brendan
Forbidden to the Duke	Liz Tyner
The Rebel Daughter	Lauri Robinson
Her Enemy Highlander	Nicole Locke

MEDICAL

Unlocking Her Surgeon's Heart	Fiona Lowe
Her Playboy's Secret	Tina Beckett
The Doctor She Left Behind	Scarlet Wilson
Taming Her Navy Doc	Amy Ruttan
A Promise...to a Proposal?	Kate Hardy
Her Family for Keeps	Molly Evans

MILLS & BOON®
Hardback – February 2016

ROMANCE

Leonetti's Housekeeper Bride	Lynne Graham
The Surprise De Angelis Baby	Cathy Williams
Castelli's Virgin Widow	Caitlin Crews
The Consequence He Must Claim	Dani Collins
Helios Crowns His Mistress	Michelle Smart
Illicit Night with the Greek	Susanna Carr
The Sheikh's Pregnant Prisoner	Tara Pammi
A Deal Sealed by Passion	Louise Fuller
Saved by the CEO	Barbara Wallace
Pregnant with a Royal Baby!	Susan Meier
A Deal to Mend Their Marriage	Michelle Douglas
Swept into the Rich Man's World	Katrina Cudmore
His Shock Valentine's Proposal	Amy Ruttan
Craving Her Ex-Army Doc	Amy Ruttan
The Man She Could Never Forget	Meredith Webber
The Nurse Who Stole His Heart	Alison Roberts
Her Holiday Miracle	Joanna Neil
Discovering Dr Riley	Annie Claydon
His Forever Family	Sarah M. Anderson
How to Sleep with the Boss	Janice Maynard

MILLS & BOON®
Large Print – February 2016

ROMANCE

Claimed for Makarov's Baby	Sharon Kendrick
An Heir Fit for a King	Abby Green
The Wedding Night Debt	Cathy Williams
Seducing His Enemy's Daughter	Annie West
Reunited for the Billionaire's Legacy	Jennifer Hayward
Hidden in the Sheikh's Harem	Michelle Conder
Resisting the Sicilian Playboy	Amanda Cinelli
Soldier, Hero...Husband?	Cara Colter
Falling for Mr December	Kate Hardy
The Baby Who Saved Christmas	Alison Roberts
A Proposal Worth Millions	Sophie Pembroke

HISTORICAL

Christian Seaton: Duke of Danger	Carole Mortimer
The Soldier's Rebel Lover	Marguerite Kaye
Return of Scandal's Son	Janice Preston
The Forgotten Daughter	Lauri Robinson
No Conventional Miss	Eleanor Webster

MEDICAL

Hot Doc from Her Past	Tina Beckett
Surgeons, Rivals...Lovers	Amalie Berlin
Best Friend to Perfect Bride	Jennifer Taylor
Resisting Her Rebel Doc	Joanna Neil
A Baby to Bind Them	Susanne Hampton
Doctor...to Duchess?	Annie O'Neil

MILLS & BOON®

Why shop at millsandboon.co.uk?

Each year, thousands of romance readers find their perfect read at millsandboon.co.uk. That's because we're passionate about bringing you the very best romantic fiction. Here are some of the advantages of shopping at www.millsandboon.co.uk:

* **Get new books first**—you'll be able to buy your favourite books one month before they hit the shops

* **Get exclusive discounts**—you'll also be able to buy our specially created monthly collections, with up to 50% off the RRP

* **Find your favourite authors**—latest news, interviews and new releases for all your favourite authors and series on our website, plus ideas for what to try next

* **Join in**—once you've bought your favourite books, don't forget to register with us to rate, review and join in the discussions

Visit **www.millsandboon.co.uk**
for all this and more today!